H. Vidaver

The Book of Life

A complete formula of the service and ceremonies observed at the death-bed,

house of mourning and cemetery

H. Vidaver

The Book of Life
A complete formula of the service and ceremonies observed at the death-bed, house of mourning and cemetery

ISBN/EAN: 9783337284558

Printed in Europe, USA, Canada, Australia, Japan

Cover: Foto ©Andreas Hilbeck / pixelio.de

More available books at **www.hansebooks.com**

ספר חחי

THE

BOOK OF LI

A COMPLETE FORMULA OF THE

SERVICE AND CEREMO

OBSERVED AT THE

Death-bed, House of Mourning and Ce

TOGETHER WITH

PRAYERS ON VISITING THE GR

ELABORATED AND REVISED BY

REV. DR. H. VIDAVER

NEW YORK:

H. SAKOLSKI, 53 DIVISION STREE

1882—5642.

PREFACE.

Sad experience has keenly made us feel the want of a practical book containing the ritual, ceremonies and customs generally observed at deaths and burials, on visiting the cemetery, and especially in the house of mourning. Any inexperienced person to whose lot has fallen the mournful task of supervising the depositing of the remains of a near relative in their final resting place, must have felt the want of a book containing the necessary instructions and directions for such occasions, in a convenient and eligible order.

Admitting that there are a number of books in existence containing such laws, usages, prayers, etc., it is an acknowledged fact that the majority of them are so badly arranged that they almost confuse a person who has not a thorough knowledge of them. To remedy this, we have arranged the present one so simply that the most inexperienced person can ascertain all information required.

We have also devoted considerable space to prayers for those visiting the graves of various relatives; the majority of which, having been originally composed by most prominent Jewish scholars, will be found more impressive and more apt to infuse the balm of consolation than the old stereotyped translations of Hebrew prayers.

The inspiration of confidence, comfort and consolation to those who have occasion to give this "BOOK OF LIFE" an attentive perusal, will be an assurance that some good has been accomplished by

THE PUBLISHER

INDEX.

·דינים·

L A W S,

Regarding the Dying, the Mourners, the House of Mourning, the
Burial Place, the Coffin, Shrouds and the Grave; the periods of
שבעה *(Shivah),* שלשים *(Shloshim),* the Anniversary of Death
(Jahrzeit), etc., etc.,—divided into 10 Sections.

SECTION I.

דיני גסיסה.

Laws concerning the Dying.

1. It being strictly prohibited to hasten the
death of man, we are therefore not allowed, (if we
will not render ourselves guilty of shedding blood) to
remove a dying person from his place, or to take from
under him the bed or any other article upon which
he lies: should he even, by our not removing him,
remain long in this awful struggle.

2. It is likewise prohibited to give to the dying
person medicine, or to apply any cure to him, when
we see that his dissolution is nigh, and that he is
past all human aid.

3. But should the sick still have sufficient
strength to drink, or should he ask, either by words
or signs, for drink, then we must give it to him.

4. Yet we are not allowed to pour it into the
mouth of the sick, lest he might choke, and we then
should have caused his death.

5. In such a crisis we must also not tear off from the sufferer anything that cleaves fast to his body: for instance, a plaster or such like.

6. Neither are we allowed to place anything beneath him, though many superstitious persons maintain that certain things, being put under the sick man's couch, will cause an easier death.

7. In case of something sticking to the lips of the sufferer, we may wipe it off, but we must be very careful not to scrape it if it sticks fast to his tongue. Should the hand or leg of the dying suspend from the bed, we may slowly and gently restore it.

8. At the time when death takes place, we must not suffer the relatives or friends to weep or cry aloud, within hearing of the dying, lest we render the struggle of death more heavy.

9. It is also strictly prohibited to speak, in the presence of the dying, of the preparations for the funeral: for by that we only increase his sufferings, by his hearing that we think already of his funeral, while he is yet alive.

On the approach of death, the prayers on page 64 are repeated by those surrounding the dying.

SECTION II.

דיני קריעה.

Laws concerning the Rending of Garments, etc.

1. The eyes of the deceased are then to be closed and the chin tied up, so that the mouth

should remain shut; and all those present at the time
when death took place, are bound to make a small
rent in one of their garments, which rent they are
allowed soon thereafter to sew together.

2.   Near relatives, who are bound to keep the
שבעה Shivah (seven days of mourning), must make a
קריעה K'reah (rent) in their garments, about the size
of a span, which is to be done in the following way.

3.   They must cut with a knife the edge of the
garment, near the neck (either in the coat or waist-
coat), and then to rend it about a span further, whilst
inclining the head over the corpse.

4.   This קריעה K'reah (rent) is to be made on the
right side of the garment, except at the death of
parents, it must be done on the left side of all garments, which the mourner just happened to have on,
with the exception of his shirt, over-coat, or mantle.

5.   The performance of this ceremony must take
place standing; and in case the קריעה K'reah (rent)
was made when sitting, we must rise, and re-perform
the same.

6.   At the death of a relative the rent may be
stitched together at the expiration of the שבעה Shivah
(seven days of mourning), and properly sewn together
after the שלשים Sh'loshim (thirty days of mourning);
except at the loss of parents, it may only be stitched
after the expiration of the שלשים Sh'loshim (thirty
days of mourning); but it must never be properly
sewn.

7.   This ceremony must be performed before the
ארון Oron (coffin) is closed.

8. It is also obligatory to make the קריעה K'reah (rent) in the garments of minors, since it is calculated to manifest signs of mourning.

9. The קריעה K'reah (rent) must be made in the front, at the edge of the garment, but not on its seam.

10. A person confined to his bed, by sickness, is exempt from making the קריעה K'reah (rent), even at the death of his parents.

11. If a person is overtaken during שבעה Shivah by the death of another relative, he tears the same קריעה K'reah (rent) made on the occasion of the first death a span further; should this, however, happen at the termination of the seven days, he has only to rend the first קריעה K'reah a small piece more, but when overtaken by the death of his parents within or soon after the שבעה Shivah (seven days of mourning) for relatives, he is then to make a new rent of the size of a span, three fingers distance from the first.

12. The laws of tearing the garments are obligatory upon every one, either male or female, with the distinction, that the latter, at the demise of parents, do not make the קריעה K'reah (rent) in the dress one above the other, on account of decency. They, therefore, must make it in different places, which rent they may afterwards stitch together.

13. At the death of an infant, less than thirty days old, neither the קריעה K'reah (rent) nor the seven days of mourning are to be observed.

14. If any of the festivals occur within the thirty days of mourning, we are exempt from all observ-

ances and customs obligatory during the thirty days, and are allowed to sew the קריעה K'reah (rent); and in case we mourn for parents, the hair of the head and the beard must not be taken off, and the rent may only be stitched together the day before the festival.

15. At the death of relatives, if we are not informed of it until after the expiration of thirty days after their demise, we are exempt from making the קריעה K'reah (rent); but, at the death of parents, we must rend all our garments we had on at the time the report reached us, though more than thirty days had elapsed since their demise.

16. One who meets with the calamity of losing both parents at once, or should the report of their demise reach him on *one* day, he makes *one* קריעה K'reah (rent) for both. But should he meet with the death of a parent and relative on *one* day, the קריעה for his parent is to be made first, and at about the distance of three fingers from the first קריעה he must make another, about the size of a span, for his relative.

17. If a sick person is taken with a fit, and the bystanders, believing him to be dead, make the usual rent, they are not bound, if he expires immediately, to re-perform the same; but if more than an hour has elasped before his demise, the rent must be again made within the width of three fingers of the first.

SECTION III.

דיני אנינות.

Laws concerning the interval between death and interment.

1. The corpse is then to be deposited on the ground, the head to be laid on a little straw, the hands and feet to be placed in a straight position; after which the whole body is to be covered with a black cloth, a lighted candle to be placed at the head, and the feet of the dead must be towards the door. The water which happened to be in the house where death occured, must be poured away.

2. People ought to be appointed carefully to watch the corpse, to prevent animals or insects touching it; and also that some one be at hand to give immediate aid, if any sign of life appear.

3. Whoever is occupied with the preparation for the funeral is exempt from the reading of the *Kereath Shemah* (שמע ישראל), and all other observances enacted by Divine Law, during the time thus occupied. Should there be many people engaged in the preparation for the funeral, they are to take the duties by turns : so that whilst one party attends to them, the other may be enabled to repeat their prayers, provided it does not in any way interfere with the funeral.

4. As long as the body is not interred, the relatives are אונים *Onim* (afflicted), and must abstain from eating meat and drinking wine until after the interment.

5. Nor need the אוֹנֵים *Onim* (afflicted), during this time (though the interment be delayed several days), say the daily prayers and blessings. They are also exempt from all ceremonial observances, including grace after meals, and the response of "Amen" to the blessings pronounced in their presence.

6. They are not to take their meals with their family at one table, but every one must take them separately. They are allowed to go out and attend to everything requisite for the funeral, and when at home they must neither take off their shoes nor sit on the ground like an אָבֵל *Ouvel* (mourner).

SECTION IV.

דיני טהרה ותכריכין.

Laws concerning the Washing and Shrouding.

1. The corpse is then placed upon the טָהֳרָה *Taharah* (purifying) board with its feet towards the door, and covered with a clean sheet. The shirt of the corpse must be rent through from the breast downward, and taken off in such a manner, so that the whole corpse should remain covered with the sheet. These ceremonial laws are even to be observed by the corpse of an infant.

2. The deceased is then to be washed with tepid water, but not with hot. We must take nine full *cabbin** of water (not less), from which we pour upon the sheet with which the corpse is covered, and was hit by the means of this sheet; but the

---

*A *cab* contains about two pints.

corpse must not be touched with the naked hand.

3. Whilst the water is thus poured over the corpse, the mouth should be covered with a clean napkin, to prevent the water from running into it. The corpse must remain covered from head to the feet during the whole time of the washing.

4. No part of the deceased body must remain uncovered which, if we were to uncover when alive, would be considered a violation of decency.

5. The washing must commence from the head, and thus downward to the feet. During the washing the corpse must lie with the face turned upwards, after which it must be inclined upon the right side, in order to wash the left side and a part of the back.

6. This being done, we are to turn it on the left side whilst the right side and the other part of the back is properly washed, and then again placed as before on the back.

7. Anything cleaving fast to the corpse need not to be scratched off. The nails of the hands and feet must be properly cleaned with pins made for this purpose.

8. After the טהרה *Taharah* (washing) is thus performed, those who attend to it are to wash their hands with clean water, and wipe them with a napkin. Four persons are to hold a clean sheet over the corpse, the lower and wet sheet on the corpse is to be removed, and other nine *cabbin* of clean and cold water are to be poured over the bare corpse, commencing from the head downwards, which is the proper and actual טהרה *Taharah* (purification).

9. The arms, feet, fingers, toes, and hair of the deceased are then to be dried by means of clean sheets. Even the board upon which the washing took place must afterwards be well cleaned and dried.

10. The טהרה *Taharah* (purifying) water spilt on the ground must be well dried. Care should be taken that the טהרה water is not poured out in public places.

SECTION V.

דיני מיתת יולדות.

Laws concerning Women dying in Child-bed.

1. If a woman die during her confinement, the above ceremony of purification by water must not be performed, if a *lochia* has taken place.

2. The דם (blood) found either on garments or on the ground, which escaped from her after her demise, must be put in a coffin, well joined and pitched.

3. Until thirty days after her confinement she is called a יולדת (woman lying-in), and in case she dies within thirty days of her confinement, all דם (blood) which came from her after her demise is called דם הנפש, (blood of the Soul) and must therefore be buried.

4. It is customary in some places, when a woman dies during her confinement with a child, to bury her in the raiment she had on at the time when death took place: viz., a linen or a common white cotton shirt is to be wrapped over the dress she happened to have on, and the usual תכריכים *Takreakim* (shrouds)

are merely put into the coffin; but she is not to
be shrouded with them.

5. In some places the תכריכים (shrouds) are put
over the dress she happened to be attired in at the
time she died. Should she die in her bed undressed,
a frock is to be put over her shirt; wrap her also in
a winding-sheet; and we may either clothe her in
the usual shrouds, or put them merely into the coffin; but we are by no means allowed to perform the
טהרה (washing).

6. Should we discover in the bed, or anywhere
else, such דם which came from her since her demise,
the place on which the דם (blood) is found must be
cut out and interred with the dead body. In some
congregations it is usual to clothe the יולדת (woman
lying-in) in her Sabbath dress and new shoes; but
the less garments she is interred with, the better it
is. We are not allowed to wash off the דם (blood),
either from the dress or from the corpse.

7. It is customary, when a woman dies during
her pregnancy, without being delivered with child,
to put at the foot of her coffin a white sheet. In
case she was delivered with child, but both die,
then the child must be washed, clothed, put in a
coffin,. and buried with the mother in one grave, but
not in one coffin.

8. It is also customary that none of the parents,
at the death of their first child, follow the funeral to
the·burial ground. We are allowed to wash the
body of one killed by accident, or one found murdered, provided we see no blood run from it. We

are also permitted to clothe the corpse in a white
shirt, over which we put the usual raiment, and then
wrap it in a white sheet. In some places it is customary to lay the תכריכים *Takreakim* (shrouds) of
a murdered person in the coffin.

SECTION VI.

דיני הרוגים.

*Laws concerning persons killed by accident, etc.; like-
wise concerning disinterment.*

1. It is usual to bury הרוגים (slain persons) at
some distance from the other graves.

A drowned person, or one dropped down dead,
from whom no blood has flowed, must be treated as
others who died naturally; he must be properly
washed, wrapped in the customary shroud, and not
in his own dress. Also if blood had run from the
body whilst yet alive, but had entirely ceased after
the demise, then the washing and clothing must be
similar to those who died naturally.

2. Should, however, blood escape from him
no טהרה (washing) must take place. We are to bury the corpse in the raiment which it had on at the
time when death took place, and everything on
which the דם (blood) ran must be cut out, even the
spot saturated with דם (blood) must be taken off
with a shovel and interred with the corpse. But
the blood which escaped from the body whilst alive,
need not be buried.

3. In such cases the coffin must be well pitched,

in order to prevent the loss of blood, since any drop of blood escaped from the deceased after the demise, must be interred.

4. The אבילות *Ovailoth* (mourning) of persons who live in a besieged town, commences from the time when the corpse is put into a coffin, shut up or fastened with screws, and placed in a bone-house, appointed to keep the dead until the raising of the siege.

5. The אבילות (mourning) for such persons whom we know certainly to have been drowned, and whose corpse cannot be found, commences from the moment when the hope of their being found is entirely given up.

6. Should the corpse, however, afterwards be found and interred, the אבלים *Ovailim* (mourners) are exempt from re-observing the שבעה *Shivah* (seven days of mourning), but the ceremony of making the קריעה *K'reah* (rent), must be re-performed; they are also obliged to observe all the אבילות (mourning) during the whole day of interment.

7. The same law is to be observed with one who was condemned to the gallows.

8. In case the corpse was not cut down until some time after the execution, the relative mourners must make again the קריעה (rent), and observe all the laws incumbent on mourners at the time of interment; but they are afterwards exempt from keeping the שבעה (seven days of mourning), or any other law obligatory upon a mourner.

9. Towards the remains of exhumed bodies

which are to be buried in another place, the same duties and respect must be paid—due to every departed.

10. They must not be disinterred before the whole flesh thereon is entirely consumed; and even then we are only allowed to do it when the departed, buried in this place, can no longer remain there, or when it was the expressed will of the departed to be afterwards dug up in order to be buried in the sepulchre of his ancestors, or in ארץ ישראל (the land of Israel, the Holy Land).

11. In case the interred bodies can no longer remain in the place where they were interred; for instance, if government do not suffer the place to be a burial ground (no difference from whatever reason), then we may disinter the remains, and carry them to some other place of rest.

12. Without any cogent reason, however, the dead are not to be disturbed in their place of repose, nor be disinterred for the purpose of assigning to them a more respectable sepulchre.

13. If the remains of several dead bodies are disinterred, care should be taken to gather the ashes of every corpse separately and not to mix them, so as to re-inter the remains of every one as they were found.

14. The bones which are yet joined, or which form a perfect skeleton, must not be dislocated.

15. The old boards of the coffin in which the corpse was deposited must not be used; they must either be buried or burnt on the same spot.

16. All ashes found, even the earth upon which the corpse laid, to the length and breadth of the grave, must be taken out, and re-interred with the remains of the corpse.

17. Children are not allowed personally to disinter the remains of their parents, nor even touch them; but they may allow others to do so.

18. The relatives who had to keep the אבילות (mourning) at the day when death took place, must re-observe it on the day of disinterment; and whatever is obligatory upon an אבל (mourner) is also binding upon them on the day of interment till nightfall, and no longer, though the remains have not yet been re-interred.

19. They are, however, exempt from observing the law of an אונן (the obligatory mourning in the interval between death and the interment).

20. If a relative hear of the disinterment of one at whose death he was bound to observe אבילות (mourning), he is equally obliged to re-observe it on the day he hears of the re-interment as on the day of death, provided he has been informed of it on the very day of the re-interment; but if later, should he even receive the information on the following day, no אבילות (mourning) takes place.

21. The relatives must perform the קריעה (rent) in their garments on the day of disinterment, and are subject to the same laws as when the קריעה (rent) was performed at the time of death.

22. It is also customary for the neighbours to send to the mourner, after the disinterment, the

סעודת הבראה (meal of condolence) as is usually done.

23. All persons occupied with the disinterment of the dead, are exempt from saying the קריאת שמע (Hear, O Israel), תפלה (daily prayer), and from putting on תפילין (phylacteries), as in case of death.

24. No כהן (descendant of Aaron) is allowed to touch the exhumed remains, not even those of his parents.

SECTION VII.

דיני תכריכין וארון.

Laws concerning the Shrouds and Coffin.

1. The deceased is clothed in the usual shrouds, according to the custom of the community.

2. Care must be taken that nothing shall be placed on the wrong side, and likewise that nothing should come to the mouth of the corpse.

3. First the מצנפת (cap or mitre) is to be put on the head, the מכנסים (breeches), then the כתונת (shirt), and next the neckcloth, and then the סרגנס (a garment for the clothing of the dead in the style of a surplice), and then the חגורה (girdle); all of which must be made of linen or common white cotton.

4. The טלית *(Tallith)* is next put on the head. One of the ציצית *Tsizith* (fringes) is to be torn. Every string or tape on the shroud must be folded twice, (but not double knotted), then twisted, and lastly, fastened into a single knot.

5. In those communities where it is customary to provide regulary made coffins a sheet is to be wrapped over the corpse as a mantle. The טלית (*Tallith*) must not be put over the head of those who were not accustomed to wear it in this way whilst they were alive.

6. No כתרה (embroidery or ornament) must be put on the טלית (*Tallith*) given to the deceased. Neither are we allowed to embroider the כנפים (corners) where the ציצית *Tsizith* (fringes) are put.

7. The ציצית *Tsizith* (fringes) are merely to be drawn into the holes of the corners, without being tied or twisted, but very simply fastened to it, so as to prevent their dropping out.

8. Should, however, some gold or embroidery be on the טלית (*Tallith*), it must be taken off, and nothing else need be substituted in its place.

9. A child that wore ציצית (fringes) whilst alive, must also be clothed in an ארבע כנפות (*Arbah Kanvoth*), from which one of the ציצית (fringes) must be torn off. But such very young children who wore no ציצית (fringes) during their lifetime, need not be clothed in it after their death.

10. No corpse must be · shrouded in less than three garments.

11. If there are sufficient persons to assist in the washing and the shrouding of the dead, no relatives, however distant, are to be engaged to do it.

12. Before the corpse is deposited in the coffin, we should measure it, in order to avoid the unneces-

sary removal of the corpse, in case the coffin is found too small.

13.   Since it is customary to make no knot in the thread with which the shrouds are sewed, care must be taken in the sewing thereof that they should not become loose in the shrouding.   It is advisable, for many laudable reasons, that every one whose situation and circumstances allow it, to prepare the customary shrouds whilst alive.

14.   We may make the shrouds of fine linen or cotton, but of no coloured or rich stuff—this would be an unnecessary expense.   The dead must also not be clothed in shrouds embroidered with silver or gold, or any other work, in order that they may not be disturbed in their place of repose, since we have had too numerous instances of graves being opened to strip the dead of their costly shrouds.

15.   Care must be taken that nothing of the shrouds should be torn or soiled.   Every hole therein must be well mended, and every spot washed out.

16.   Should it, however, happen that they become soiled after having been put on the corpse they must be washed, though they become wet thereby.

17.   The sewing of the shrouds is to be done by daughters of Israel with pious zeal.   It is to be performed from a motive of tender mercy, from truly good and unselfish feelings towards the departed.

18.   No woman during her castamenia is allowed to assist in washing and clothing of the dead.

19.   Also females must not be shrouded in less than three garments; viz., a short קיטל (surplice)

and a sheet wrapped over the corpse as a cloak. Besides these shrouds, it is customary to clothe the corpse of females in a cap, stockings, girdle, and collar.

20. An infant one year old must also be clothed in shrouds the same as an adult; but if less than one year old no סרגום (surplice) is required. If the infant was yet swaddled whilst alive, the same must be done after its death. We are to clothe it in a shirt, then wrap it in a sheet, over which the corpse is to be bandaged. Also the legs are to be wrapped in a piece of cotton or linen. But if the infant was not bandaged when alive, then it is only to be clothed in a shirt, סרגום (surplice) and girdle.

21. The corpse of a נפל (premature birth) is only to be wrapped in a sheet. Infants who die soon after birth, must be shrouded in a shirt and sheet, provided they have already been dressed in the former when alive.

22. The corpse being thus washed and shrouded, is next to be put into the coffin, the legs must be placed together in a straight position. The thumbs must be put into the palm of the hand, encompassed by the other four fingers, and in order that the thumbs should not come out from their proper places, they are to be tied with the ציצית Tsizith (fringes) of the טלית (Tallith). The wrapping of the corpse in the sheet must be done in such a manner that the collar of the shirt should not come into the mouth.

23. Also the knees of the corpse are to be well covered with the winding-sheet or סרגום (surplice),

which is to be drawn over the legs, and in case it is too long it must be drawn up and folded under the girdle.

24. The hands are to be placed at the side in a straight position, between the coffin and the body, in such a way that any motion or shaking, caused by the removal of the coffin, might not remove them from their proper position.

25. The coffin is then covered with a black cloth, the foot of it towards the door through which it is to be carried, and lighted candles at the head thereof.

SECTION VIII.

דיני חדר שמת מונח בו.

Laws concerning the chamber where the corpse lies.

1. In the chamber where the מת (corpse) lies, we are neither allowed to perform the daily prayers (תפלה), or to study the law. Persons desirous of doing so must quit the room, even on שבת Sabbath or יום טוב (the festival days).

2. Those who have no other room save that where the מת (corpse) is deposited, must erect a partition to screen it.

3. Sermons and moral reflections, however, are allowed to be delivered in the room where the corpse is deposited.

4. All garments taken off from the deceased may again be used.

5. The hair cut off from the deceased by urgent necessity, must be interred with it.

6. False hair worn by the departed may again be used.

7. Should it, however, have been tied to, or twisted in the hair of the departed, then it must be used by none, unless the deceased, whilst alive, particularly desired it to be given to one of her friends to wear.

8. The hair cut off whilst alive need not be interred with the departed.

9. In a word, everything separated from the body during life, and which grows again, for instance, teeth, hair, nails, &c., need not be put with the departed into the grave.

10. Some, however, preserve the teeth fallen out from them in an age when they grow no more, in order to be interred with them.

11. Limbs cut off by medical operation or by accident must be buried immediately.

12. Shrouds prepared for the funeral may be used for any other purpose, provided they were as yet not put on the corpse. In these cases the shrouds prepared for the מת (departed) must be unripped.

13. The same is to be observed when a grave has been dug, and another is afterwards fixed upon, the former must be filled up. Also when some hindrance occurs, so that the funeral cannot take place on the day appointed, then the grave must be filled up or covered, and must not be left open over night.

SECTION IX.

דיני נטיאת המת לֹקבוּרה.

Laws concerning the conveying of the dead to the burying-ground, etc.

1. The corpse is to be carried to the grave, the coffin covered with a black cloth, followed by the mourners, and joined by the procession.

2. No relative is to assist in carrying the מטה (bier) to the grave, when there are others to do it.

3. We are also permitted to follow the funeral of those persons with whom we were at variance during their lifetime, save the deceased protested against it in his last will, or verbally expressed himself that this or that person should not follow his funeral.

4. The לוּיה (funeral procession) must be performed with propriety and order. The followers must manifest their participation, and the whole of the ceremony must bear the stamp of solemn order. Persons behaving themselves with wanton levity on such an awful occasion, by laughing and profane jesting, do not only offend the dead, but disgrace themselves and debase humanity.

5. Without cogent reasons, the corpse must not be kept long uninterred.

6. We are, however, allowed to leave the corpse uninterred longer than usual, when it is calculated for the honour and respect due to the departed; for instance, to wait for absent relatives or friends, or to procure things indispensable for the funeral, or

even to be enabled to do it with more honour and
propriety, or to avoid unlawful proceedings. In these
cases we are allowed to keep the corpse one or two
days, BUT NOT LONGER.

7. No corpse is allowed to be conveyed from
one community to another, when the former has a
burial ground of its own, save when the deceased
has expressed in his last will a particular wish to be
carried to the place of the sepulchre of his ancestors.

8. Children are in duty bound carefully to ar-
range the solemn funeral of their departed parents,
and are likewise to bear all the expense necessary
for the interment, though no inheritance whatever
was left to them.

9. It is customary to have a מצבה *Matsaivah*
(tomb) set at the expiration of one year from the
day when death took place; in some countries the
מצבה (tomb) is set after the שלשים *Sh'loshim* (thirty
days of mourning), and sometimes even within that
period (the thirty days after death).

SECTION X.

דיני אבילות, שבעה, שלשים, וכו'.

*Laws concerning Mourning, its beginning, its observa-
tion during the Shivah, Sh'loshim etc., etc.*

1. After the interment has taken place, the usual
time of אבילות (mourning) commences. The mourners
must neither sit upon a chair or bench, but upon the
ground, they are however permitted to use some low

seàts (such as mats or hassocks), but they must not
sit upon rich cushions or pillows.

2. After the return from the burial place, the
mourners are to read the customary daily prayers,
provided the time for the reading of the *Shemah*
is not yet expired, but they must not put on the
תפילין *T'filin* (phylacteries).

3. It is customary that the neighbours of the
mourners send them, after the interment of their
departed relatives, some food, which consits of hard-
boiled eggs and bread, termed סעודת הבראה (meals of
condolence).

4. At this first meal neither wine or meat must
be used, both may, however, be taken by the mourner after the above-mentioned meal.

5. During the שבעה *Shivah* (the seven days of
mourning), the mourner must not wear shoes, nor
transact any business, and must also avoid every
sexual intercourse. Mourners occupied in the
study of other religious books, are only to choose
such passages applicable to mourning, or such passages as bear upon it.

6. In case the mourner needs to leave the room,
he may put on the shoes, which he is again to take
off immediately after his re-entering the room. Persons to whom the taking off of the shoes might prove
injurious, are allowed to put on worn out shoes or
slippers.

7. It is customary not to allow persons to sleep
on the bed or on the couch on which the deceased
expired, during the whole שבעה *Shivah* (seven days

of mourning). They also suffer none to sit on the chair on which the departed used to sit. A most praiseworthy custom indeed, calculated to keep in reverence the memory of our departed friends or relatives.

8. For the following seven relatives we are bound to keep the שבעה *Shivah* (seven days of mourning), and observe all the ceremonies stated above: at the death of a father or mother, son or daughter, brother or sister, either by father or mother (older than thirty days), and at the death of a husband or wife.

9. No אבילות *Ovailoth* (mourning) is incumbent upon males less than thirteen years old, and upon females less than twelve years old. They need not, therefore, sit upon the ground at the departure of one of the above enumerated seven relatives, though they may enter into this age during the שבעה *Shivah* (seven days of mourning).

10. At the death of parents, or even of young children, as well as of adults, we dress in black, for black is סימן אבילות (a badge of mourning).

11. Persons overtaken within a שבעה *(Shivah)* with the death of another of the above seven relatives, need not keep separate seven days, but commence the second שבעה *(Shivah)* from the interment of the second relative, and continue to keep the seven days.

12. No business must be transacted by the אבלים *Ovailim* (mourners) during the seven days of mourning. They are, however, permitted to write letters, provided their contents are of a strictly private nature, and cannot well be confided to others.

13. Cooking and baking for their own use may
be done by the mourners themselves; also the rinsing
and washing of utensils, and the cleaning of the
house, the making of the beds, and the washing of
linen for little children.

14. Poor persons, who are compelled to work
for their daily maintenance, may work privately after the expiration of three days of the שבעה *Shivah*
(seven days of mourning), in order to procure their
daily maintenance.

15. Servants in mourning are allowed to do any
kind of work; but it is very just and equitable that
their employers should allow them an hour or half
an hour daily, in which they might sit upon the
ground, and observe the customary ceremonies.
Such services which can be done without interrupting
the earnestness of mourning, servants in mourning
are bound to do.

16. Teachers may instruct their pupils after
three days of the שבעה. Children in mourning may
go to be instructed.

17. We are not allowed to put on the usual Sabbath dress on the Sabbath within the שבעה. It is very
commendable for the mourner, during the whole
twelve months, to be attired in black, for the reason
stated above: viz., that black is אבילות סימן (a badge
of mourning). It is, therefore, usual to put a black
עטרה on the טלית; and on Sabbath, when no mourning is to be observed, the טלית is to be turned on
the other side, or folded.

18. Mourners summoned to appear before a

court of justice, or before any other authority, may go without any hesitation or scruple.

19. The business of such mourners who are in partnership with others, may be carried on privately by the latter after the first three days, though the former profits by it.

20. Whoever deals in an article for which there is a momentary demand, and which, if not sold immediately, might cause a loss, or if the mourner can purchase an article which must be bought at once to prevent loss or its being damaged, is permitted to have such articles sold or bought for him by others, but not in his own house.

21. No אבל *Ouvel* (mourner) is allowed to wait during the thirty days of mourning on tables where there is music. Those who mourn for the death of their parents are prohibited from doing the above during the whole twelve months of mourning.

22. But when there is no music at the table the mourner may act as waiter, after the שלשים *Sh'loshim* (thirty days of mourning), when mourning for parents; and even within the שלשים when mourning the loss of other relatives.

23. In a like manner the mourners for parents are not to visit parties and feasts during the whole year; and when mourning for other relatives, they are only to abstain from it during the שלשים.

24. Poor musicians who are in mourning may play at banquets and feasts, even during the thirty days, but if mourning for their parents they are only allowed to do it after the שלשים. It is a matter of course that they are only permitted to do it in order

to provide their daily necessaries, but by no means
when tending to their amusement.

25. Physicians and surgeons may, even within
the שבעה, attend on their patients who are in need of
their medicial assistance, though there are in the
same place other professional men to do it.

26. During the whole thirty days no mourner is
permitted either to bathe or to anoint himself, or to
take off the beard, or to pare the nails, both from
the hands and feet. Persons in mourning for parents ought to wear the beard during the whole twelve
months; but when their business compels them to
mix among people, may only then take off the beard
when they call attention to their ill-looking and al-
tered appearance.

27. If the thirtieth day of שלשים Sh'loshim (thirty
days of mourning) fall on Friday, the mourner needs
no more, on account of the honour due to Sabbath,
observe the rites, laws, and ceremonies connected
with the שלשים.

28. Every mourner should, at the demise of relatives, change his usual seat at the public place
of worship during the whole שלשים, and at the demise of parents he is to change it during the whole
year.

29. The sitting upon the ground for our departed
relatives ought to be as far as possible in the room
where death took place.

30. It is customary to have during the whole
שבעה Shivah (seven days of mourning) a lighted lamp
in the place where the deceased ended his earthly

life; the reason of which is aptly derived from the verse, "The soul of man is the lamp of the Eternal." Prov. xx. 27.

31. Mourners who celebrate a בְּרִית מִילָה *B'rith milah* (circumcision), within the שִׁבְעָה, are permitted to go to the synagogue, but they are not allowed to take off the beard or to have their hair cut, nor to change their dress.

32. They must neither provide any feast whatever, but are merely to invite ten persons מִנְיָן *(Minyan)*, to partake of something, in order to be enabled to repeat the בִּרְכַּת הַמָּזוֹן *Birchath hamoson* (grace after meals); after which the mourners are again to observe every ceremony and law incumbent upon them.

33. The mourner is also permitted to perform the duties of מוֹהֵל *(Mohel)*, when there is no other besides him, even on the first day of the שִׁבְעָה; and as soon as the operation is over he must go directly from the synagogue to his house, and is not to partake of the סְעוּדָה *Soodah* (meal generally provided on such occasions).

34. In like manner may the mourner, after the expiration of three days of the שִׁבְעָה be a "*Gevatter*" (godfather); he must say the daily prayer at home, attend synagogue whilst the circumcision takes place, and then return to his house to sit upon the ground as an אָבֵל, and is likewise not to partake of the סְעוּדָה *Soodah* (banquet.)

35. Every mourner may during the שְׁלֹשִׁים *Sh'loshim* (thirty days of mourning) accept the office of

a מוהל *(Mohel)* and "*Gevatter*" (godfather), and may also partake of the meal generally given on such occasions. He may wash, bathe, and change his dress, but those who mourn for the death of parents are only allowed to do it after the שלשים.

36. Should the mourner himself be the בעל ברית *Bal b'rith* (the father of the child to be circumcised), though he bewails the loss of his parents, he is still permitted to wash, bathe, and change his dress, even within the שלשים, but he must not take off his beard.

37. The mourner may also accept the office of an "*Unterführer*" (the giver away of a bride or bridegroom), but he must not attend the dinner, or enjoy the music on such occasions; and when mourning for a parent, he may only accept it after the שלשים, when he is allowed to take off his beard, and also put on his Sabbath dress, which he may wear until the marriage ceremony is concluded. He may also act as בעל ברכה (reader of the blessings pronounced under the חופה *Huppah*), but he must by no means attend the banquet or music on such occasions during the whole twelve months.

38. Persons in mourning, who give away a female orphan, may, when the marriage happens to take place within the שלשים *Sh'loshim* (thirty days of mourning), attend the wedding house, in case their presence is required, but they must not partake of the banquet, and when they mourn for parents they are only allowed to do it after the שלשים.

39. Neither males or females are to be betrothed during the שבעה.

40. Bachelors and spinsters in mourning may be betrothed within the שלשים, and marry after the שלשים, when they are permitted to dance and participate in every entertainment as any other bride or bridegroom who are not in mourning; but as soon as the wedding week is over, they are again to put on their mourning dresses, and observe every law incumbent upon mourners.

41. Parents in mourning, celebrating the marriage of their daughters, are allowed to do everything at the wedding, as if they were not in mourning, but they are to take care not to exceed the limits of rational enjoyment; and soon after the wedding day they are again to put on their mourning apparel.

42. One who has lost his wife must not marry again until the expiration of the annual שלש רגלים *Sholosh r'golim*: viz., Passover, Pentecost and Tabernacle. ראש השנה *Rosh Hashono*, (the New Year), and יום הכפור *Yom hakkippur*, (Day of Atonement), are not termed רגל (festival), and are therefore not to be included therein.

43. It is incumbent upon all who mourn for the loss of their wives, to observe all the ceremonies and laws of an אבל *Ouvel* (mourner) during the שלשים.

44. If the bride or bridegroom unfortunately lose one of their parents on the wedding day, when everything necessary for such an occasion was prepared, so that by a delay of the wedding they might incur a great loss, they are permitted to go under the חופה *Huppah* (to be married), and also תשמש המטה, after which the corpse of the deceased is to

be interred. The new couple have to observe, as all other newly married who are not mourners, the בבת ימי המשתה (the seven days of joy), at the expiration of which they must keep the שבעה *Shivah* (seven days of mourning). The thirty days of mourning commence from the first day of the שבעה, inasmuch as they have previously observed no אבילות whatever.

45. But in case the bridegroom wishes to observe the seven days of mourning, previous to his wedding, he is allowed to do it, and the nuptials may take place as soon as the שבעה is over. But when one of the parents dies after the marriage ceremony has taken place, the mourning bride or bridegroom must observe the שבעה soon after the interment.

46. In regard to the laws incumbent upon mourners, no distinction is to be made between male or female.

47. When the going without shoes is injurious to the health of a female, she need not take them off.

48. Females are likewise to wear mourning-dresses during the whole year.

49. A woman who has lost her husband must remain in her widowhood for three months and a few days; and in case she had a child by her deceased husband, which was not yet weaned, she is not allowed to re-marry until the child is two years old. During her widowhood she is to wear mourning the whole year, as at the loss of parents.

50. A woman whose husband has gone away, without her knowing what has become of him, or if

her husband be drowned, and the corpse not identi-
fied, she is called a עגנה, and is to observe no אבילות
Ovailoth (mourning) whatever, nor are the children
allowed to say קדיש *(Kaddish)*.

51. At the demise of distant relatives, for whom
no שבעה *Shivah* (seven days of mourning) is to be
observed, we are at least bound to keep some אבילה,
in abstaining from feasts during the whole שבעה,
even at the ברית מילה *B'rith milah* (circumcision) of
grand-children. We are in like manner to wear on
the first Sabbath some of our weekly garments.

52. At the death of מחותנים (people related by
marriage) no אבילות whatever takes place. Alike, if
we are informed of the death of one of our distant
relatives, thirty days after their demise, no אבילות
is to be observed, save the usual custom to wear on
the first Sabbath some of our daily garments.

53. It is customary for the mourner, on the eve
of the Sabbath within the seven days, to go to the
synagogue, at the entrance of which he remains
during the מנחה *Mincha* service, and before the reader
commences the Psalm of מזמור שיר ליום השבת, the שמש
calls out מנחם אבלים (condolence to the mourners),
and then they are brought into the Synagogue by
the Rabbi or by the minister.

54. On the Sabbath of the שבעה no אבל *Ouvel*
(mourner) is to be called up to the reading of the
law. The same is to be observed with an אונן who
attends synagogue on Sabbath or on the festivals,
he must not be called up.

55. In case the אבל is a כהן *Cohen*, and there

be no other besides him, or if he were called up by mistake, he may then be כולה להודה (go up to the reading of the law); he is, however, not allowed to repeat the פרשה (portion) read to him, but merely to listen to it.

56. He, the כהן, must likewise quit the synagogue during the whole שלשים, when the כהנים go to דוכן (to recite the sacredotal blessings), and when mourning for parents he is to observe it during the whole year; also a מוהל *Mohel*, godfather, or בעל ברית the father of the circumcised child, must not be called up during the שבעה *Shivah* (seven days of mourning). But הוצאה והכנסה the taking out and replacing of the scroll, or הגבהה וגלילה, the lifting up and rolling thereof, the אבל may perform.

57. When the last day of the שבעה falls on the Sabbath, the mourner need not to sit on the ground at מוצאי שבת *Mozai Shabbath* (the exit thereof); for the שבעה ends with the termination of the morning service. If it happen to fall on any day in the week, the mourner has only to sit *one* hour on the ground, and then the שבעה is terminated.

58. If any one die on Sabbath, we are not permitted to close the eyes neither to tie up his jaws, nor to straighten his hands and feet on that day; but we are allowed to prevent the mouth from being more opened than it was at the time when death took place. Care, however, must be taken not to draw the jaws together, or to close the mouth more than it was בשעת מיתה (at the time he died).

59. If the deceased is to be removed on Sabbath

from the bed where he died, in order to be deposited
on the ground (generally called *Abheben*), a small
loaf must be placed on the corpse, which must remain on it during its removal ; neither are we permitted to have a burning candle placed at its head
until the termination of Sabbath.

60. In the above-mentioned case the אונן may
partake of meat and wine, perform the daily service,
and even attend Synagogue. In some communities
no אונן attends the place of worship, even on Sabbath.
If he perform the Sabbath prayer at his own house,
he must neither repeat מגן אבות nor מדליקין במה.

61. At the exit of Sabbath, the אונן is to read the
evening service, מעריב *(Mahrib)*, somewhat earlier
than any other individual: for as soon as night has
set in he must read no prayer whatever, nor even
pronounce the ברכת הבדלה. The latter, however,
must be repeated by the mourner after the interment, provided it does not exceed Tuesday; he then
repeats the blessing over a glass of wine, but neither
the customary בשמים (spices) nor the light are to be
used at its performance. The mourners for those
persons who died on ערב יום טוב, the day before the
festival, when there was no time to inter the corpse
before יום טוב *Yom Tove* (the festival days), are permitted to attend synagogue, to perform the service
of the day, and may drink wine, eat meat, and repeat the ברכת המזון *Birchath hamoson* (grace after
meal), אבל אסורים בתשמיש המטה. Moreover, though
the departed is only to be interred after יום טוב, the
אנינות (mourning) incumbent before the interment
does still not commence till the day on which the

preparations are made for the burying, and the mourners are therefore allowed, during the whole יום טוב to eat meat and drink wine, and perform the daily service, and at the exit of ירו טוב, they have to observe the same laws as at the exit of the Sabbath. In this case nothing must be done for the interment until after יום טוב, not even by a non-Israelite.

62. The same law is to be observed when persons die on the eve of פסח. The mourners may partake of meat and wine, but the סדר (service on the eve of Passover) must be performed by another, to which they are to listen attentively, but not to repeat, and they must likewise partake of the מצה *Mazzah* and מרור *Moror*, and afterwards repeat the הלל *Hallel*. They must also not make הכבה (couch), and put on כרנים (surplice), where it is customary to do it: mourners for parents are to abstain from the last two ceremonies during the whole year.

63. When the departed are to be brought to their place of repose on the morrow of the first day of יום טוב *Yom Tove* (the festival days), the אוננים may attend the place of worship on the eve previous, and may also occupy their usual seats, perform the daily service, and are permitted to partake of meat and to repeat grace after meals. The corpse may be removed on יום טוב from the bed where death took place, in order to have it deposited on the ground, without laying a loaf on it, as is done on Sabbath. We are in like manner allowed to close the eyes and tie up the jaws of the deceased, and place a burning candle at the head, and cover it with a black cloth.

64. All manner of work which we are prohibited to do on the Sabbath, must likewise not be performed for the funeral on the first day of יום טוב; we may, however, warm the water for the טהרה *Taharah* (purification); carry the departed to the burial-ground, provided the latter is בתיך ההתום, but not by hearse, carriage, or ship. The latter, however, may be done without scruple by those who are not Israelites, save no יהודי sits in the carriage or goes on board the ship to attend the funeral; the latter, however, may follow it on foot, when it is בתוך התחום. The making of the coffin, the digging of the grave, the depositing of the coffin into it, and the filling up thereof, must be done by a non-Israelite; but in case there is none to untertake it, the corpse must remain uninterred until the following day, when the depositing of the coffin into the grave may be done by Israelites, who are also allowed to carry back every tool necessary for the interment to the place where they are generally kept.

65. No nail or screw is to be driven into the coffin on יום טוב *Yom Tove* (the festival days), but we may put them into the hole made for that purpose. No napkin must be torn, or any other thing broken, though it be necessary for the funeral. In a like manner must the shirt not be torn off from the deceased before the טהרה, as it is the custom on a working day, neither are the mourners to make קריעה.

66. In some communities no funeral takes place on the first day of יום טוב, because we might then not be enabled to treat the deceased according to the laws, rites, and customs; or that a profanation

of the holiday might ensue, save in such cases where
the corpse might through this delay remain too long
uninterred.

67. The טהרה taking place on יום טוב is to be performed in the following manner: the corpse is to be
placed on the טהרה board, a white sheet is to be
covered over it, the shirt of the deceased is to be
taken off in such a way that the whole corpse should
always remain covered with the sheet, over which
sufficient water is to be poured to wet the whole
corpse, and whilst the water is thus poured a napkin
must be held over the mouth of the deceased, to
prevent the water from running into it. We are,
also, to take more water than usual, and pour it
from the head to the heel, since the corpse must not
be washed by the sheet on יום טוב, as on a common
day. The nails, both of the hands and feet, are to
be well cleaned, but care must be taken not to
scratch off from the corpse anything that cleaves
fast to it. Having thus proceeded, water is again
to be poured over the corpse; but we must by no
means wash or rub it with the sheet.

68. Respecting the shrouding of the corpse, we
are to proceed as at other טהרות; but nothing must
be scratched off from the body. Care must likewise
be taken to dry the corpse well.

69. To perform the טהרה on יום טוב by means of
straw or hay, as suggested by many, is, for several
well grounded reasons, not to be approved of. In
case a funeral takes place on יום טוב, very early in
the morning, care ought to be taken that those per-

sons who follow the funeral shall not neglect the morning service.

70. It is laudable and preferable in every respect to make the לויה after the morning service is over, in order that none might be prevented from attending the funeral procession, nor run the risk of neglecting the morning service.

71. The mourners have to observe no אבילות (mourning) whatever, they may go, as every non-mourner, from the burial ground to the synagogue, attend worship, where they need not change their seats, neither are they to mark their טלית *Tallith* with a black ribbon, אבל אסורים בתשמיש המטה. Their mourning commences with the termination of the holidays, when they are to keep the seven days.

72. If the festival terminate on the eve of Sabbath, the mourners are not brought to the synagogue by the ministers before the chaunting of מזמור שיר ליום השבת, since no mourning has yet been binding upon them. At the exit of Sabbath they must make the קריעה *K'reah* (rent) in their garments, and also sit upon the ground, which is accounted for a whole day; and on the ensuing Thursday, after the mourners have sat a short while upon the ground, the שבעה is completely ended.

73. The שלשים commence from the day of interment. The same laws which are to be observed at funerals on the first day of יום טוב *Yom Tove* (the festival days) are alike to be regarded on the second day, with the distinction that if on the second day we cannot meet with a non-Israelite to undertake

the necessary requisites for the funeral, Israelites may perform it; they may therefore make the coffin, cut and sew the shrouds; may also ride or go on ship, even beyond the החום, and make the grave as on a working day. But all this must be performed in private as much as possible, carefully avoiding to excite public attention.

74. In this case things ready-made are to be preferred, though they be inferior to those that were to be made new; and all that can be done by ONE person, must not be performed by two or more.

75. In case the corpse is to be conveyed in a hearse or ship beyond the החום, it must be followed by no more persons than those necessary for the interment; and even parents are, in this case, not to follow the funeral of children, and *vice versa*.

76. If the death of a person who requested in his last will to be buried in the sepulchre of his fathers, happen to be on יום טוב, though there be a burial-ground in the place where he died, he must, nevertheless, be conveyed after יום טוב to the place where he requested to be buried; but if the corpse cannot remain longer uninterred, it must be buried at the same place where death took place, but when the deceased can be kept until after יום טוב, he must be conveyed to the place where he requested to be buried; for it is incumbent upon every one to comply with the desire of the deceased, as much as it lies in our power, provided it is not against religion.

77. When non-Israelites undertake to prepare the necessary requisites for the funeral, on the sec-

ond day of יום טוב, all must be done by them as · on
the first day.

78. Those Israelites whose attendance cannot be
dispensed with at the interment, are allowed to follow the funeral by ship, even beyond the תחום,
though non-Israelites are the undertakers; they are
also permitted to fill up the grave after the coffin
was deposited into it, which is, however, in no way
permitted to be performed by Israelites on the first
day of a festival. Thus we see that on the first day
of festivals everything necessary for the interment
must be performed by non-Israelites, and when such
are not to be met with to undertake it, the corpse
must not be buried on that day, whilst on the second
day of יום טוב Yom Tove (the festival days), when
non-Israelites refuse to undertake the funeral preparations, Israelites are allowed to perform everything, as well as on a working day.

79. Shrouds becoming soiled after their having
been put on the deceased on the first day of a festival, are only to be well dried with a towel, but on
the second day of יום טוב the stain may be washed
out with cold water, but not with warm; and though
the shrouds become wet, the corpse need still not
be disrobed of them, in order to have them well
cleaned. It is therefore very essential to put a napkin upon the mouth of the deceased, to prevent the
shrouds from being soiled in case of exudation.

80. We must not inquire after the price of those
things purchased on יום טוב for the interment of the
dead. The amount must be paid after the holidays;

but we are permitted to give a pledge or a security, even on the second day of יום טוב. We are not allowed, on that account, to let the corpse remain uninterred, but in case of need we may even on the second day of יום טוב buy everything necessary for the funeral, even for ready money, and also saw the boards for the coffin, and perform everything necessary for the funeral.

81. A premature birth, or a child born dead, נפל בוודאי, must be buried neither on the first nor on the second day of יום טוב. A child who dies on יום טוב soon after birth, or should it even die on the thirtieth day after birth, ספק נפל, may only be buried when we are aware that it was maturely born: viz. when the child has hair and nails; but in case it was a male child that was not yet circumcised, we are not allowed to bury it until after יום טוב, since the circumcision must be operated on the dead body on the burial-ground before the interment, which operation must not be performed either on the first or second day of יום טוב.

82. Also if an infant more than thirty days old die, which had not yet been circumcised, it must alike not be buried until after יום טוב, on which day the circumcision before the interment must likewise be performed. This operation is to be done by means of a sharp piece of glass, but not with a knife or any other instrument. The ערלה is to be thrown into the grave. No פריעה takes place, neither is the usual blessing to be pronounced before the operation, and it may also be performed by one who is not a מוהל.

83. The relatives of those persons who die on חול המועד are called אוננים until after the interment has taken place, and have to observe no אבילות *Ovailoth* (mourning) until after אבל אסורים בתשמיש : ויום טוב המטה. And although they need not observe publicly the ceremonies of mourning, they are, nevertheless, bound to observe privately every duty of a mourner. They are therefore to avoid every merriment, and must also not be called up to the reading of the law, but הוצאה והכנסה (the taking out of the scroll from, and the restoring the same to the ark) they may have. And though, as mourners, they are prohibited from studying the law, they are nevertheless permitted to read a certain portion, or a chapter, which they usually have appointed as their daily task.

84. Masters or tutors who are אבלים *Ovailim* (mourners), on חול המועד are without any scruple allowed to instruct their pupils.

85. Mourners must make no קריעה *K'reah* (rent) on חול המועד, though they bewail the loss of parents, until after יום טוב. In some communities, however, they make the קריעה on חול המועד for the loss of parents. ויהי נועם and בלע המות are to be repeated after the interment, even on יום טוב. On שבת חול המועד the mourners may attend synagogue, but they are not brought into it by its ministers, previously to the chaunting of מזמור שיר ליום השבת.

86. Since no אבילות is to be observed on חול המועד, mourners are, therfore, to read the daily prayer, at the performance of which they are to put on their תפילין *T'filin* (phylacteries), provided the interment

takes place before the time fixed for the reading of
the morning service has passed.

87. If a funeral takes place on ערב יום טוב (the
day previous to the festival), so late in the day that
the mourners have not time to sit a short while on
the ground before the commencement of יום טוב,
they must, after the holidays, observe six ·days to
complete the שבעה Shivah (the seven days of mourning). The שלשים Sh'loshim (thirty days of mourning), however, commence immediately after the
interment. But if the departed was buried, and
there was yet a short time left for the mourners to
sit upon the ground before the commencement of
יום טוב, the festival takes off the whole שבעה.

88. The same law is to be observed in those
communities where it is customary to fasten the
coffin in the house where death takes place, without
re-opening it on the burial-ground, when the approaching festival clears the whole שבעה, after the
mourners have sat a short while upon the ground,
immediately after the coffin was removed from the
house, though the interment did not take place till
late at night, and we were obliged to engage non-
Israelites for its completion.

89. But when the mourners follow the funeral to
the burial-ground, the mourning does not commence
until after the interment was thoroughly over.

90. Though the מעריב Mahrib (evening service)
was read in the public place of worship by the whole
community before night has set in thoroughly, except by the mourners, who have only a few minutes

left to them to sit upon the ground before night, the
almost approached festival does, nevertheless, exon-
erate them from keeping the שבעה. The same is
the law when the coffin is nailed up in the dying-
chamber, with a view not to re-open it on the
burial-ground, on account of its distance from the
residence of the mourners, in which case the mourning
alike commences soon after the coffin was removed
from the house.

91. If the last day of שבעה fall on ערב יום טוב (the
day before the festival), the customary thirty days
of mourning (שלשים) are considered terminated on
that day, and the mourners are therefore permitted
to do on ערב יום טוב everything prohibited to mourners during the שלשים. But in case the departed
was interred on ערב יום טוב, on which occasion the
mourners commenced their שבעה, though only a
short time (about half an hour) before the commencement of the festival, the mourners are then exempt
from the duties of the שבעה but are bound to keep
the שלשים.

92. When the last day of the שבעה happens
on ערב פסח (the day preceeding the Passover festival), the mourners are allowed to have their beards
taken off (except when they mourn for parents), and
to bathe even before noon, which they are not permitted to do on another ערב יום טוב until the afternoon.

93. In case the mourners sat a short time before
the commencement of a festival upon the ground,
and thus began the שבעה, the approaching holiday

exempts them from observing the שבעה, and clears likewise eight days from the שלשים; the mourners have therefore only to observe, after the festival, fifteen days more, in order to complete the thirty days of mourning.

94. If the mourners commenced their אבלה on the day before the New Year (ראש השנה ערב) the New Year takes off the seven days, and the subsequent יום הכפור Yom hakkippur (the Day of Atonement) clears the שלשים.

95. The same is to be observed when the mourners commenced their שבעה on כפור יום ערב; the Day of Atonement clears the שבעה, and the succeeding סוכות (the festival of Tabernacles) takes off the שלשים.

96. And though the thirty days of mourning are not yet completed, the mourners are still allowed to wash and bathe, on account of the honour due to the approaching festival.

97. If the mourners commenced to observe the אבלות Ovailoth (mourning) on סכות ערב, though only a short time before the commencing of the festival, this hour is to be accounted for seven days; the seven days of the festival likewise take off seven other days, which make fourteen days; to this we add the subsequent שמיני עצרת, which also clears seven days; and the last day, viz., שמחה תורה, is likewise to be reckoned for one day, which altogether amount to twenty-two days. Hence the mourners have only to observe, after the holidays, eight days more, to complete the שלשים.

98. Though in the above cases the mourner is

exempt from observing the usual laws of mourning, he is still entitled during the whole seven days after the interment to every קדיש at the morning and evening service, with the exception, when there are solemnizing the anniversary of the death of parents, in which case the קדשים are to be accordingly allotted.

99. If the sixth day of the שבעה occurs on ערב יום טוב, the approaching holiday takes off the whole שבעה and a part of the שלשים; the mourners must not have their beards taken off until the end of the thirty days, neither are they permitted to put on their shoes, or to go out from the house, before noon. The mourner may attend synagogue at the afternoon service, into which he is not to be brought by its ministers, but he must change his usual seat.

100. Those who lament the loss of parents, must neither bathe nor have their beard taken off on ערב יום טוב, though the festival clears the שלשים. They are, however, allowed to pare their nails, and also to change their linen.

101. If the last day of the שבעה occurs on ערב שבת, which happens to be before ערב יום טוב, the festival takes off both the שבעה and שלשים. Should, however, the sixth day of the שבעה occur on Friday, then the approaching holiday clears the whole שלשים; but he must not have his beard taken off until after יום טוב, inasmuch as the שבעה was not completed before its entrance. Such mourners, however, are allowed to have their beards taken off on חול המועד, with the exception when mourning for parents.

102.   In case the thirtieth day of the שלשים happens on Friday, the mourners are allowed to have their beards taken off in the afternoon.

103.   Mourners are allowed to attend the כלי ההני on ערב ראש השנה and ערב יום הכפור even in the midst of the שבעה. A mourner is only then allowed to perform the service on ראש השנה ויום הכפור (viz., to be a בעל תפלה or חזן), if there is not another to be had in the same community capable of performing it, or if the other is much inferior to the mourner.

104.   No reader is to mark the Taleth in which he performs Divine service during the year with a black ribbon, called כברה.

105.   Those who mourn for one who died on ערב השעה באב (the 8th of the month Ab), are called אוננים, and are as such prohibited from performing the usual daily prayers; neither are they permitted to attend synagogue at the evening and morning service to hear the reading of the איכה Aichoh (Lamentations of Jeremiah). After the reading of the morning service, the interment may soon take place, but neither צדוק הדין nor the קדיש (Kaddish), repeated at funerals, are to be said. If the interment was completed before the expiration of the time set apart for the reading of the morning service, the mourners must repeat it as usual, after which they are to sit on the ground.

106.   The מנחה Mincha (afternoon service) the mourners are to say somewhat later, at the performance of which they are to put on their תפילין (phylacteries). Mourners are allowed to attend syna-

gogue on the 9th day of the קינות *Kinoth* (elegies)
and the איכה, but not longer, from whence they are
to return directly to their house, and observe every
law obligatory on mourners during the whole שבעה.

107. The mourners of those who die on חנוכה
Chanuckah are likewise before the interment called
אוננים, and are therefore not allowed to kindle the
usual חנוכה lights, nor are they permitted to repeat
the daily prayers. At the interment neither the
הצור תמים nor the קדיש, generally repeated at funerals,
are to be recited; as soon as the interment has
taken place, the mourners have to observe the שבעה.
They are, however, to have the חנוכה lights kindled
by others, and to repeat אמן after the blessing.

108. In case the time appointed for the reading of
the morning prayers was not yet over on their return
from the funeral, they are to be repeated by the
mourners, but they must not put on the תפילין; and
on the night subsequent to the interment they are to
kindle the חנוכה lights. If a מנין is convened in the
house of mourning during the שבעה on הנוכה or ראש
חדש *Rosh Chodesh*, the mourners are to quit the
room whilst the הלל is read, though less than ten
persons remain in it.

109. Funerals which take place on ערב הנוכה, both
the צדוק הדין and קדיש are to be repeated, even in
the afternoon.

110. Funerals taking place on the day before
Purim (תענית אסתר) the mourners are to read the
evening prayers at their own residence, and may only attend the place of worship during the reading of

the מגילה *Meggillah* (Book of Esther). On the subsequent morning they may remain at the place of
worship both during the whole service and the reading of the מגילה (the Book of Esther); but they must
not occupy their usual seats, neither observe any
public mourning until after the feast of Purim,
אבל אסורים בתשמיש המטה. We are alike prohibited
from sending to the mourner the usual שלוח מנות,
but we may send him צדקה *Tzdoko* (charity), in case
he is in need of it. The אבל is, however, permitted
to send שלוח מנות to two persons, and charity to as
many as he can afford.

111. If a person die on ערב פורים so late that the
relatives are not able to inter him on the same day,
they are to repeat their prayers at home, attend
synagogue during the reading of the מגילה. אבל אסורים
בתשמיש המטה, and are also prohibited from partaking
of meat and wine; the same law they have to observe on the subsequent morning service, after which
the interment is to take place, but neither the צדוק
הדין *Ziduck Hadin* nor the usual קדיש is to be said;
and in case the interment takes place before the
expiration of the time appointed for the service, the
mourners are to repeat it without putting on the
תפילין *T'filin*.

112. On the two days of Purim no public mourning is to be observed, which are still counted for
two days, and at the evening of שושן פורים the mourners are to resume the שבעה and complete it.

113. The mourners for those persons who die on
Purim, that could not be interred on the same day,

are at the סעודת פורים *Soodath Purim* (the banquet given on Purim) allowed to partake of meat and wine; it is a matter of course that they must not drink it to excess and intoxication, but must be mindful and conscious of the loss they have sustained. The mourners must on that day make no preparation whatever for the interment. In case the burial-ground is a great distance from the place where the corpse lies, so that the mourners are compelled to make the arrangements for the funeral early on that day, they are to read the מגלה afterwards, though the time for the reading of the morning service has elapsed.

114. If the report of the death of a relative reach us within thirty days after his demise, it is called a שמועה קרובה (recent report); and a שמועה רחוקה (an old report) signifies when we are informed of the loss of our relatives after thirty days of their demise.

115. At a שמועה קרובה we are to observe every ceremony of mourning, both as regards the rending of the garment קריעה *K'reah* (the rent), and those of the שבעה *Shivah* (seven days of mourning) and the שלשים *Sh'loshim* (thirty days of mourning); the two latter commence from the day the report reached us. In a word, the day of a שמועה קרובה though we were informed of it on the thirtieth day, is in every respect equal to the day when the death of a relative took place. In case a person was informed of it before, and he has not yet repeated the evening prayers, though they were already said in the synagogue, the mourner is only to sit a few minutes upon the ground, which is accounted for a day.

116. But if he (the mourner) has already said the מעריב *Mahrib* (evening prayers) at the time when the report reached him, though it had not yet been read in synagogue, he is at once to sit upon the ground; but the seven days commence only from the subsequent day, when he is to read his morning prayers without the תפילין *T'filin*.

117. The same is the case when the sad report reaches the mourner on ערב שבת or on ערב יום טוב, before he has recited the evening prayers, and there is yet time left to sit a few minutes upon the ground before night, though the evening prayers were already finished in the synagogue, these few minutes are still to be reckoned for a whole day, and the almost approached holiday clears the whole שבעה.

118. But if the report reaches the relative so late in the day that there was no time left for him to sit upon the ground before night, the holiday does not clear the שבעה.

119. At the termination of יום טוב he must commence the שבעה; but the שלשים he commences from the day the report reached him, ואסור בתשמיש המטה עד אחר יום טוב.

120. But if he is informed of the death of a relative after thirty days of the demise, the mourner need only sit upon the ground *one* hour, but he is exempt from making the קריעה, neither do we send him the סעודת הבראה (meal of condolence), and both the שבעה and שלשים are terminated, after having sat one hour upon the ground.

121. But if he hear of the death of a father or

mother, though it be after thirty days of their demise, the mourner is still bound to perform the קריעה,
to sit one hour upon the ground, and to observe the
שלשים, which commence from the day when the report reached him.

122. Persons who are informed of the death of
their parents in the twelfth month after their demise,
need only sit one hour upon the ground. Previous
to their sitting upon the ground they are to perform the קריעה, observe the שלשים, and the (*Jahrzeit*)
anniversary of their death they are to keep, in common with their other brothers and sisters who were
present at the death of their father or mother. They
are likewise not to say קדיש *Kaddish* until the
Jahrzeit (anniversary).

123. Persons who are informed of the death of
their relatives, after the expiration of the year of
mourning, are exempt even from sitting one hour
upon the ground, and are free from observing every
law and ceremony incumbent upon mourners.

124. But if he hear of the demise of his parents,
though it be after the year of mourning was completed, he is still to make the קריעה, and to sit *one*
hour upon the ground; but he is exempt from all
other אבילות, and is even not to say the קדיש, except
on the *Jahrzeit* (anniversary), which he is to solemnize in common with his other brothers and sisters.

125. The *Jahrzeit* (anniversary) is always to be
solemnized on the day when the death took place.

126. The קדיש is only to be repeated by the
mourners during eleven months, whilst all other

ceremonies of mourning are to be observed during the whole twelve months.

127. It is customary to fast on the anniversary (*Jahrzeit*) of the death of parents, and if it happen on a day when the prayers of תחנון are not said, we need not to solemnize it by fasting.

128. We are *not to participate in any feast or banquet* on the eve previous to the anniversary (*Jahrzeit*). If the first anniversary occur on Friday, and we did not, on account of the Sabbath, fast until night, then we are exempt from fasting the whole day on subsequent years, though it does not fall on Friday; but if we fasted the first year the whole day, we are then to observe it afterwards.

129. It is also customary to have a candle or lamp burning from the eve of the anniversary to the other, in commemoration of the honour due to departed parents; and when persons die without children, this practice ought to be carried out by the relatives.

130. In case the death of a relative occur in the month of אדר, in a common year (שנה פשוטה), the anniversary is to be observed in the following year in the same month, viz., אדר ראשון, though it be a שנה מעוברת (an embolismic year); but should the demise of a relative happen in a שנה מעוברת (embolismic year), the anniversary is always solemnized in אדר שני (second month of Adar); for the anniversary is always to be observed in the same month that death took place. The קדיש for our departed parents is only to be repeated by the mourners for eleven months from the time when death took place, provided not

more than one day intervenes between death and
interment; hence persons who, die on the fifth of the
month of כסן, in a common year, but the ensuing
year is a שנה מעיברת (an embolismic year), the
mourners are to say קדיש till the fifth of אדר ראשון
(first Adar). The twelve months of mourning terminate on the fifth day of the second Adar, and on
the fifth day of the month of Nisan (which is the
thirteenth month) the anniversary is to be solemnized, for the reason stated above, viz., that the
anniversary is always to be observed on the same
day of the month that death took place.

131. The *Jahrzeit* (anniversary) of those persons
who die on אדר שני is to be solemnized in every subsequent embolismic year in אדר שני, on the same day
when death took place.

132. The relatives of those persons who die on
the first day of ראש חדש *Rosh Chodesh*, are to keep the
anniversary in every subsequent year on the same
day; and in case it takes place on the second day of
ראש חדש, the mourners have to solemnize the anniversary on the second day of ראש חדש.

133. If a person die on the second day of ראש חדש,
but the subsequent year of that month has only one
day ראש חדש, the anniversary is to be kept on the
day of ראש חדש.

134. Some are accustomed to keep the anniversary
of those who die in אדר (embolismic year), both in
אדר ראשון and אדר שני.

135. In case we are not certain of the anniversary,
we are allowed to choose any day in the year, which

day is afterwards to be solemnized as the anniversary; but we are not entitled to repeat קדיש, in case there are other mourners in synagogue.

136. לדוד ברוך and למנצח בנגינות are to be chanted at מוצאי שבת, in the house of mourning, within the שבעה, and the prayer אנא ה' (generally recited after the delivery of the discourse) is not to be repeated on those days when תחנון is not said.

137. Mourners are permitted to repeat the ברכת לבנה (blessing said on the appearance of the new moon), when the time set apart for that service expires before the termination of the שבעה.

138. No כהן must touch the remains of his sister by his mother's side, though she had been single, nor is he permitted to be in the room where the corpse lies.

סדר התפלות׃

The following prayer is to be recited by a person conscious of the approaching hour of death.

אָנָּא יְיָ אֱלֹהִים אֱלֹהֵי יִשְׂרָאֵל חַי וְקַיָּם נוֹרָא

וּמָרוֹם וְקָדוֹשׁ, אַתָּה אֲשֶׁר בְּיָדְךָ נֶפֶשׁ כָּל־חָי וְרוּחַ

כָּל־בְּשַׂר אִישׁ, מוֹדֶה אֲנִי לְפָנֶיךָ שֶׁבְּרָאתַנִי וְנָתַתָּ

בִּי נִשְׁמָתִי, וְהִגְדַּלְתַּנִי וְהִצַּלְתַּנִי מִכָּל־צָרוֹתַי, וְנָתַתָּ

לִי כָּל־צָרְכֵי מְזוֹנוֹתַי וּפַרְנָסָתִי כָּל־יְמֵי חַיַּי וְהָיִיתָ

עִמָּדִי וְלֹא עֲזַבְתָּנִי . הִנֵּה הִגִּיעָה הָעֵת וְהָעוֹנָה

שֶׁאַחֲזִיר לְךָ נִשְׁמָתִי אֲשֶׁר נָתַתָּ בִּי : קַח אוֹתָהּ

מִמֶּנִּי עַל־יְדֵי נְשִׁיקוֹת פִּיךָ וְלֹא עַל־יְדֵי מַלְאֲכֵי

מָוֶת וְאַל־יְבַהֲלוּנִי לְצַעֲרֵנִי, תַּסְתִּירֵנִי בְּצֵל כְּנָפֶיךָ,

וְכַאֲשֶׁר גָּמַלְתָּ עָלַי חַסְדְּךָ וַאֲמִתְּךָ מְעוֹדִי עַד־הַיּוֹם

הַזֶּה כֵּן גְּמָל־נָא עָלַי חֶסֶד וֶאֱמֶת עִם־גּוּפִי וְנִשְׁמָתִי

וּשְׁלַח־לִי מַלְאָכֶיךָ הַקְּדוֹשִׁים לְקַבֵּל נִשְׁמָתִי

לְהוֹלִיכָהּ לְגַן עֵדֶן אֶל־נִשְׁמוֹת הַצַּדִּיקִים וְהַחֲסִידִים.

וְגוּפִי יָנוּחַ בַּקֶּבֶר בִּמְנוּחָה נְכוֹנָה בְּהַשְׁקֵט וְשָׁלוֹם

עַד עֵת בּוֹא דְּבָרְךָ לְהַחֲיוֹתוֹ בִּתְחִיַּת הַמֵּתִים:

ORDER OF PRAYERS.

The following prayer is to be recited by a person conscious of the approaching hour of death.

I beseech Thee, Almighty God! God of Israel, who art everlasting and immutable, awfully sublime and holy. In Thy hands are the souls of all living, and the spirits of all flesh of man. I humbly acknowledge before Thee, that it is Thou who hast created me, and breathed within me the breath of life; it is Thou who hast reared me, and delivered me from all my troubles; it is Thou who hast provided for me in all my wants, my sustenance and maintenance, during all the days of my life. Yea, it is Thou who wast always with me, and never forsookest me. The moment has now arrived at which I have to return to Thee the soul which Thou hast deposited within me. O Creator of all! mayest Thou receive back from me this sacred deposit in mercy and peace, and may its departure be neither disturbed or affrighted by the vision of the angel of death. O, hide me in the shade of Thy wings; and as Thou hast dealt with me in Thy mercy and in Thy truth, from my existence until this day, so do Thou, even now, bestow Thy compassion and truth upon my body and soul. I beseech Thee, send Thy angels of mercy and truth to attend the last moment of my existence, to receive my soul, and to restore her to her heavenly source—the garden of Eden, in the celestial circle of the departed pious and righteous, and may my body also rest in the grave in peace and quietude.

וּתְהִי תְשׁוּבָתִי וְצַעֲרִי וּמִיתָתִי כַּפָּרָה עַל־כָּל־חַטֹּאתַי

שֶׁחָטָאתִי וְשֶׁעָוִיתִי וְשֶׁפָּשַׁעְתִּי לְפָנֶיךָ בִּהְיוֹתִי עַל־

אַדְמָתִי, כִּי הִסְכַּלְתִּי כִּי עָשִׂיתִי וְהַשְּׂאוֹר שֶׁבְּעִסָּתִי

הִשִּׁיאָנִי: וְאַל־תַּרְאֵנִי פְּנֵי גֵי־הִנֹּם, וְתֵן חֶלְקִי בְּגַן

עֵדֶן עִם־צַדִּיקֵי עוֹלָם וְאֶזְכֶּה לִתְחִיַּת הַמֵּתִים וְלָעוֹלָם

הַבָּא שֶׁכֻּלּוֹ שַׁבָּת לְהִתְעַנֵּג מִדֶּשֶׁן נַפְשִׁי וּמֵרֹב טוּב

הַצָּפוּן לַצַּדִּיקִים בְּשֵׁ׳׳י עוֹלָמוֹת אֲשֶׁר תַּנְחִיל לְכָל־

צַדִּיק וְצַדִּיק מֵעַמְּךָ יִשְׂרָאֵל, כַּכָּתוּב לְהַנְחִיל אֹהֲבַי ׀

יֵשׁ וְאֹצְרוֹתֵיהֶם אֲמַלֵּא וּתְהִי נַפְשִׁי צְרוּרָה בִּצְרוֹר

הַחַיִּים עִם שְׁאָר צַדִּיקִים וְצִדְקָנִיּוֹת בְּגַן עֵדֶן אָמֵן

סֶלָה:

The following verses are to be pronounced distinctly and solemnly
by those who surround the death bed, seeing that life is departing.

יְיָ מֶלֶךְ יְיָ מָלָךְ יְיָ יִמְלוֹךְ לְעוֹלָם וָעֶד :

בָּרוּךְ שֵׁם כְּבוֹד מַלְכוּתוֹ לְעוֹלָם וָעֶד :

(ג׳ פעמים)

יְיָ הוּא הָאֱלֹהִים : (ז׳ פעמים)

שְׁמַע יִשְׂרָאֵל יְיָ אֱלֹהֵינוּ יְיָ אֶחָד :

ויכוונו ליציאת נשמתו באחד :

O may my sincere repentance, my affliction, my death, be an atonement for all my sins by which I have sinned, offended and trespassed before Thee during my earthly pilgrimage. For, verily, I have acted foolishly; my evil inclination has beguiled me; O God, doom not my soul to perdition, but grant me a portion in the garden of Eden, in the assembly of the saints and pious ones. Deign that I may be worthy of participating in the resurrection of the dead, and in the tranquil bliss of a future world, which is a one and everlasting Sabbath—when my soul will feast on that abundance of good which Thou hast laid up with Thee as an inheritance for the righteous; as vouchsafed by Thy sacred word: "I will cause my friends to inherit everlasting substance; and their treasures I will fill." And may my soul be bound up in the bundle of life, and enjoy everlasting happiness with the pious and saints in the garden of Eden. Amen.

The following verses are to be pronounced distinctly and solemnly by those who surround the death bed, seeing that life is departing.

THE ETERNAL REIGNETH, THE ETERNAL HATH REIGNED, THE ETERNAL SHALL REIGN FOR EVER AND EVER.

BLESSED BE THE NAME OF HIS GLORIOUS KINGDOM FOR EVER AND EVER. *(Repeat three times)*.

THE ETERNAL IS THE ONLY GOD. *(Repeat seven times)*.

HEAR, O ISRAEL, THE ETERNAL IS OUR GOD, THE ETERNAL IS ONE.

The bystanders should be mindful that the words ‏ה׳ אהד‏, (signifying the All-merciful God, who is *one* and eternal), should be repeated at the very moment when the sufferer expires.

Before depositing the corpse on the floor (which is generally done an hour after death) the following verses are repeated:

בֵּית יַעֲקֹב לְכוּ וְנֵלְכָה בְּאוֹר יְיָ : אֵל וֹ אֱלֹהִים יְיָ
דִּבֶּר וַיִּקְרָא־אָרֶץ מִמִּזְרַח־שֶׁמֶשׁ עַד־מְבוֹאוֹ : יָבוֹא
שָׁלוֹם יָנוּחוּ עַל־מִשְׁכְּבוֹתָם : כִּי־עָפָר אַתָּה וְאֶל־
עָפָר תָּשׁוּב :

When pouring the water on the corpse, the following verses are recited.

וַיִּצֹק מִשֶּׁמֶן הַמִּשְׁחָה עַל רֹאשׁ אַהֲרֹן וַיִּמְשַׁח
אֹתוֹ לְקַדְּשׁוֹ : כִּי בַיּוֹם הַזֶּה יְכַפֵּר עֲלֵיכֶם לְטַהֵר
אֶתְכֶם. מִכֹּל חַטֹּאתֵיכֶם לִפְנֵי יְיָ תִּטְהָרוּ : וְזָרַקְתִּי
עֲלֵיכֶם מַיִם טְהוֹרִים וּטְהַרְתֶּם מִכֹּל טֻמְאוֹתֵיכֶם
וּמִכָּל גִּלּוּלֵיכֶם אֲטַהֵר אֶתְכֶם : וִהְיִיתֶם קְדוֹשִׁים
כִּי קָדוֹשׁ אֲנִי יְיָ :

טַהֲרָה. טַהֲרָה. טַהֲרָה :

When the cap is put on the head of the deceased, the following verse is said:

וַיָּשֶׂם אֶת הַמִּצְנֶפֶת עַל רֹאשׁוֹ :

When the corpse is put into the coffin, the following is said:

עַל מְקוֹמוֹ יָבוֹא (לנקבה עַל מְקוֹמָהּ תָּבוֹא) בְּשָׁלוֹם :

Before depositing the corpse on the floor, (which is generally done one hour after death), the following verses are repeated:

O house of Jacob, come, we will walk in the light of the Eternal. The Omnipotent Eternal God hath spoken and proclaimed to the earth, even from where the sun riseth to the place where it sets: "peace shall come, and they shall be at rest in their place of repose; for dust thou art, and unto dust shalt thou return."

When pouring the water on the corpse, the following verses are recited:

And he poured of the anointing oil upon the head of Aaron, and he anointed him to sanctify him. From this day He (God) will atone for you to purify you; from all your sins ye shall be cleansed before the Eternal. And I will pour upon you pure water, and ye shall be cleansed; from all your uncleanliness and abomination will I purify you. And ye shall be holy, for I, the Eternal your God, am holy.

Purification! Purification! Purification!

When the cap is put on the head of the deceased, the following verse is said:

And he put the mitre upon his head.

When the corpse is put into the coffin, the following is said:

May [he] [she] go to [his] [her] appointed place in peace.

Before removing the corpse from the house of mourning to the
burial ground, the following prayer is recited by the minister or
any other person:

אֵל אֱלֹהֵי הָרוּחוֹת, נוֹתֵן לְכָל חַי נְשָׁמָה, מֵכִין
תֵּבֵל בְּחָכְמָה, תּוֹלֶה אֶרֶץ עַל בְּלִי מָה, אַתָּה בּוֹחֵן
כָּל לֵב, וְאֵין נִסְתָּר מִנֶּגֶד עֵינֶיךָ, אַתָּה עוֹז לָנוּ יוֹם
וָלֵיל, וְחַיֵּינוּ הֵם בְּיָדֶיךָ, כַּךְ נֶחְשֶׁה תָמִיד, וְלֹא נִירָא
שׁוֹד וָפֶגַע, בְּחַסְדְּךָ נַשְׂכִּיל וְנַצְלִיחַ, וְלֹא יְאוּנֶה
אֵלֵינוּ נֶגַע, בִּרְצוֹנְךָ נַעֲלֶה מָעְלָה, בִּרְצוֹנְךָ נֵרֵד
מַטָּה, וּבִרְצוֹנְךָ נָשִׁיב לָךְ הַנְּשָׁמָה לָנוּ נָתַתָּ. מִי
כָמוֹךָ אֱלֹהִים מְחַיֶּה כָּל יְצוּרִים, מִי כָמוֹךָ סוֹמֵךְ
נוֹפְלִים וּמַתִּיר אֲסוּרִים: בְּהִתְעַטֵּף עָלֵינוּ רוּחֵנוּ
בְּעֵת צָרָה וְתוֹכֵחָה, עֵינֵינוּ רַק לָךְ נְשׂוּאוֹת וּתְפַלְּטֵנוּ
לָךְ עֲרוּכָה. כְּבוֹא מָוֶת אַכְזָרִי לְהַכּוֹת מַכָּה נִצַּחַת
לִטְרוֹף טֶרֶף מִקִּרְבֵּנוּ, וְשָׁלְלוּ מִמִּשְׁפַּחְתֵּנוּ לָקַחַת,
אוֹ עָנָן וַעֲרָפֶל יְכַסּוּ מוֹשְׁבוֹתֵינוּ וְקוֹל תַּאֲנִיָּה וַאֲנִיָּה
נִשְׁמַע בְּמַחֲנֵנוּ, רַק אֵלֶיךָ אֵל עוֹנֶה בַּצַּר, נִקְרָא
מִן הַמֵּצַר, וְאַתָּה מִשָּׁמַיִם תִּשְׁלַח לָנוּ נוֹחַם, וְעֶזְרָה
מִצַּר: גַּם עַתָּה בְּבֵית אֵבֶל זֶה נִתְפַּלֵּל אֵלֶיךָ אָנָּא
חַזֵּק נֶפֶשׁ הָאֲבֵלִים, שְׁלַח לָמוֹ נֶחָמָתְךָ יַכִּירוּ וְיֵדְעוּ
כִּי דַיָּן אֱמֶת הִנֶּךָ.

Before removing the corpse from the house of mourning to the burial ground, the following prayer is recited by the minister or any other person.*

Almighty God! Lord of all flesh and all spirits, Creator of the universe, Sustainer of all with wisdom and grace! Thou triest man's heart, and nothing is hidden from Thine all-seeing eye; Thou art our tower of strength by day and by night; and our lives are in Thy hand. Through Thy mercy we prosper; through Thy will we die. Thou commandest, and we return Thee our soul which Thou hast given us. Who is like unto Thee, Preserver of all creatures? Who, like Thee, supports the fallen, and frees the enthralled? Whenever our spirits are wrapt in gloom; whenever a day of wrath and visitation cometh, we raise our tearful eyes in prayer to Thee, and crave Thy love and mercy. When cruel death makes his appearance in our abodes and snatches away one of those whose heart is bound up with ours, and thus spreads darkness and desolation in the midst of our families: O then, heavenly Father, we lift up our afflicted hearts to Thee, invoking Thy paternal help and Thy consolation; for Thou alone canst console us.

Thus, merciful God, even now, in this house of mourning we humbly beseech Thee: grant Thy consoling and sanctifying spirit to these mourners; grant that they may be able to bear their trial with spiritual fortitude and trust in Thee. May they fully comprehend that Thou art a " Righteous Judge."

---

* This prayer, in Hebrew and English, is an original composition of Rev. Dr. VIDAVER, Rabbi of the Congregation *B'nai Jeshurun*, New York.

וְאֶת נִשְׁמַת פלוני תִּצְרוֹר בִּצְרוֹר הַחַיִּים, בֵּין
נַפְשׁוֹת הַצַּדִּיקִים שׁוֹכְנֵי שָׁמַיִם . אָמֵן :

On the arrival of the funeral at the burial ground, the coffin is
placed on the bier, and the following prayers are solemnly recited.
(At the burial of infants, less than thirty days old, these prayers
are not said).

בָּרוּךְ אַתָּה יְיָ אֱלֹהֵינוּ מֶלֶךְ הָעוֹלָם אֲשֶׁר יָצַר
אֶתְכֶם בַּדִּין. וְזָן וְכִלְכֵּל אֶתְכֶם בַּדִּין. וְהֵמִית אֶתְכֶם
בַּדִּין. וְיוֹדֵעַ מִסְפַּר כֻּלְּכֶם בַּדִּין. וְעָתִיד לְהַחֲזִיר
וּלְהַחֲיוֹתְכֶם בַּדִּין: בָּרוּךְ אַתָּה יְיָ מְחַיֵּה הַמֵּתִים:

אַתָּה גִבּוֹר לְעוֹלָם אֲדֹנָי מְחַיֵּה מֵתִים אַתָּה רַב
לְהוֹשִׁיעַ מְכַלְכֵּל חַיִּים בְּחֶסֶד מְחַיֵּה מֵתִים בְּרַחֲמִים
רַבִּים סוֹמֵךְ נוֹפְלִים וְרוֹפֵא חוֹלִים וּמַתִּיר אֲסוּרִים
וּמְקַיֵּם אֱמוּנָתוֹ לִישֵׁנֵי עָפָר: מִי כָמוֹךָ בַּעַל גְּבוּרוֹת
וּמִי דוֹמֶה לָּךְ מֶלֶךְ מֵמִית וּמְחַיֶּה וּמַצְמִיחַ יְשׁוּעָה.
וְנֶאֱמָן אַתָּה לְהַחֲיוֹת מֵתִים:

הַצּוּר תָּמִים פָּעֳלוֹ כִּי כָל־דְּרָכָיו מִשְׁפָּט. אֵל
אֱמוּנָה וְאֵין עָוֶל. צַדִּיק וְיָשָׁר הוּא: הַצּוּר תָּמִים
בְּכָל־פֹּעַל. מִי־יֹאמַר לוֹ מַה־תִּפְעָל. הַשַׁלִּיט בְּמַטָּה

And may it be Thy sacred will to accept the soul of the dear departed, (*N. N.*), into the abode of everlasting bliss, among the souls of the pious and righteous, the dwellers of heaven, the inheritors of eternity.   Amen.

On the arrival of the funeral at the burial ground, the coffin is placed on the bier, and the following prayers are solemnly recited. (At the burial of infants, less than thirty days old, these prayers are not said).

Blessed be the Eternal God, King of the universe, who formed you in *justice*, maintained and supported you in *justice*, who caused you to die in *justice*, who knoweth the number of all of you in *justice*, and who is prepared to resuscitate you in *justice*.   Blessed art Thou, O Eternal, the reviver of the dead.

Thou, O Eternal, art mighty for ever: it is Thou who revivest the dead, and art mighty to save. Thou maintainest the living by mercy, quickenest the dead with great mercy: supportest the fallen, and healest the sick: Thou releasest the captives, and art ready to accomplish Thy faith unto those who slumber in the dust.   Who is like unto Thee, O mighty Lord? or who can be compared unto Thee? O King, who orderest death, and restorest to life, and causest salvation to spring forth.

God, the Rock, His deeds are perfect; for all His ways are just.   He is the God of truth, and without iniquity; He is just and righteous.   He is the Rock of all perfection—perfect in all His works :—who can say, What doest Thou—to Him who ruleth above

וּבְמַעַל. מֵמִית וּמְחַיֶּה. מוֹרִיד שְׁאוֹל וַיָּעַל: הַצּוּר

תָּמִים בְּכָל־מַעֲשֵׂה. מִי יֹאמַר־לוֹ מַה־תַּעֲשֶׂה. הָאוֹמֵר

וְעֹשֶׂה. חֶסֶד חִנָּם לָנוּ תַעֲשֶׂה. וּבִזְכוּת הַנֶּעֱקַד

כְּשֶׂה. הַקְשִׁיבָה וַעֲשֵׂה: צַדִּיק בְּכָל דְּרָכָיו הַצּוּר

תָּמִים. אֶרֶךְ אַפַּיִם וּמָלֵא רַחֲמִים. הַמָּלֵא־נָא וְחוּס־

נָא עַל אָבוֹת וּבָנִים. כִּי לְךָ אָדוֹן הַסְּלִיחוֹת

וְהָרַחֲמִים: צַדִּיק אַתָּה יְיָ לְהָמִית וּלְהַחֲיוֹת. אֲשֶׁר

בְּיָדְךָ פִּקְדוֹן כָּל־רוּחוֹת. חָלִילָה לְךָ זִכְרוֹנֵנוּ לִמְחוֹת.

וְיִהְיוּ נָא עֵינֶיךָ בְּרַחֲמִים עָלֵינוּ פְּקֻחוֹת. כִּי לְךָ

אָדוֹן הָרַחֲמִים וְהַסְּלִיחוֹת: אָדָם אִם בֶּן־שָׁנָה יִהְיֶה.

אוֹ אֶלֶף שָׁנִים יִחְיֶה. מַה־יִּתְרוֹן לוֹ. כְּלֹא הָיָה יִהְיֶה.

בָּרוּךְ דַּיַּן הָאֱמֶת. מֵמִית וּמְחַיֶּה: בָּרוּךְ הוּא. כִּי

אֱמֶת דִּינוֹ. וּמְשׁוֹטֵט הַכֹּל בְּעֵינוֹ. וּמְשַׁלֵּם לְאָדָם

חֶשְׁבּוֹנוֹ וְדִינוֹ. וְהַכֹּל לִשְׁמוֹ הוֹדָיָה יִתֵּנוּ: יְדַעֲנוּ יְיָ

כִּי צֶדֶק מִשְׁפָּטֶךָ. תִּצְדַּק בְּדָבְרֶךָ. וְתִזְכֶּה בְשָׁפְטֶךָ.

וְאֵין לְהַרְהֵר אַחַר מִדַּת שָׁפְטֶךָ. צַדִּיק אַתָּה יְיָ

וְיָשָׁר מִשְׁפָּטֶיךָ: דַּיַּן אֱמֶת שׁוֹפֵט צֶדֶק וֶאֱמֶת.

בָּרוּךְ דַּיַּן הָאֱמֶת. שֶׁכָּל־מִשְׁפָּטָיו צֶדֶק וֶאֱמֶת: נֶפֶשׁ

and beneath, who taketh away life and giveth it,
and bringeth down to the grave and raiseth up there-
from? He is the Rock—perfect in all His works:
who shall say unto Him, What doest Thou? Thou,
who promisest and fulfillest, show Thy gracious
mercy unto us; and for the sake of him who was
bound on the altar like a lamb, O hearken to our
supplication, and grant our request. Thou, who
art righteous in all Thy ways, Rock of perfection,
long-suffering, and abundant in mercy, we beseech
Thee, have pity and compassion on us, and spare
both the fathers and the children; for unto Thee, O
Eternal, appertains compassion and forgiveness.
Righteous art Thou, O Eternal, in taking away or
giving life; for in Thy hand are deposited all spirits.
Far be it from Thee to blot us from memory. O let
Thine eyes be open towards us in mercy; for Thou
art the Lord of compassion and pardon. If a man
liveth one year, or he liveth a thousand years, what
availeth it? for, is he not as though he had never
been? Blessed be the true Judge, who taketh away
and giveth life: blessed be He, for His judgments
are true: and with His eye He surveyeth all things,
and rewardeth man according to his works. Let all
men therefore praise His name. We know, O Eternal, that Thy judgments are righteous; Thy judgments are pure, none shall presume to question Thy
justice. Righteous art Thou, O Eternal! and righteous are Thy judgments. Thou art the true Judge:
for all Thy judgments are founded on truth. Blessed
be Thou, the true Judge: for all Thy judgments are
just and true. The soul of every living creature is

כָּל־חַי בְּיָדֶךָ. צֶדֶק מָלְאָה יְמִינְךָ וְיָדֶךָ. רַחֵם עַל־
פְּלֵטַת צֹאן יָדֶךָ. וְתֹאמַר לַמַּלְאָךְ הֶרֶף יָדֶךָ: גְּדֹל
הָעֵצָה וְרַב הָעֲלִילִיָּה אֲשֶׁר עֵינֶיךָ פְקֻחוֹת עַל־כָּל־
דַּרְכֵי בְּנֵי אָדָם. לָתֵת לְאִישׁ כִּדְרָכָיו וְכִפְרִי מַעֲלָלָיו:
לְהַגִּיד כִּי־יָשָׁר יְיָ. צוּרִי וְלֹא־עַוְלָתָה בּוֹ: יְיָ נָתַן
וַיְיָ לָקָח. יְהִי שֵׁם יְיָ מְבֹרָךְ: וְהוּא רַחוּם יְכַפֵּר עָוֹן
וְלֹא יַשְׁחִית וְהִרְבָּה לְהָשִׁיב אַפּוֹ וְלֹא יָעִיר כָּל־
חֲמָתוֹ:

_____

When carrying the corpse to the grave, the following psalm is
repeated several times:

יֹשֵׁב בְּסֵתֶר עֶלְיוֹן בְּצֵל שַׁדַּי יִתְלוֹנָן: אֹמַר לַיהֹוָה
מַחְסִי וּמְצוּדָתִי אֱלֹהַי אֶבְטַח־בּוֹ: כִּי הוּא יַצִּילְךָ
מִפַּח יָקוּשׁ מִדֶּבֶר הַוּוֹת: בְּאֶבְרָתוֹ יָסֶךְ לָךְ וְתַחַת
כְּנָפָיו תֶּחְסֶה צִנָּה וְסֹחֵרָה אֲמִתּוֹ: לֹא־תִירָא
מִפַּחַד לָיְלָה מֵחֵץ יָעוּף יוֹמָם: מִדֶּבֶר בָּאֹפֶל יַהֲלֹךְ
מִקֶּטֶב יָשׁוּד צָהֳרָיִם: יִפֹּל מִצִּדְּךָ אֶלֶף וּרְבָבָה
מִימִינֶךָ אֵלֶיךָ לֹא יִגָּשׁ: רַק בְּעֵינֶיךָ תַבִּיט וְשִׁלֻּמַת
רְשָׁעִים תִּרְאֶה: כִּי־אַתָּה יְהֹוָה מַחְסִי עֶלְיוֹן
שַׂמְתָּ מְעוֹנֶךָ: לֹא־תְאֻנֶּה אֵלֶיךָ רָעָה וְנֶגַע לֹא־

in Thy hand: for righteousness filleth Thy right hand. O have mercy on the remnant of Thy flock, and say unto the angel: withdraw thy hand. O Thou, who art great in counsel and mighty in deeds, whose All-seeing eye is open upon the ways of the children of men, to give every one according to the fruits of his works—to manifest that the Eternal is upright: He is my Rock, in whom there is no iniquity. The Eternal hath given, and the Eternal hath taken away; blessed be the name of the Lord. But He, the most merciful, forgiveth iniquity, and destroyeth not; but often turneth aside His anger, and awakeneth not all His wrath.

When carrying the corpse to the grave the following psalm is repeated several times:

He who dwelleth in the secret place of the Most High, shall abide under the shadow of the Almighty. I say unto Thee, the Eternal is my refuge and fortress, my God, in whom I trust. He will surely deliver thee from the fowler's snare, and from the destructive pestilence. He will cover thee with His pinions, and under His wings shalt thou take refuge; His truth shall be thy shield and buckler. Thou shalt not be afraid of the terror of the night nor of the arrow which flieth by day; nor of the destruction that wasteth at noon-day. A thousand shall fall at thy side, and a myriad at thy right hand; but unto thee it shall not come nigh. Thou shalt only behold it with thine eyes, and see the retribution of the wicked; because thou hast made the Eternal, who is my refuge, even the Most High, thy stronghold. No

יְקָרֵב בְּאָהֳלֶךָ: כִּי מַלְאָכָיו יְצַוֶּה־לָּךְ לִשְׁמָרְךָ בְּכָל־
דְּרָכֶיךָ: עַל־כַּפַּיִם יִשָּׂאוּנְךָ פֶּן־תִּגֹּף בָּאֶבֶן רַגְלֶךָ:
עַל־שַׁחַל וָפֶתֶן תִּדְרֹךְ תִּרְמֹס כְּפִיר וְתַנִּין: כִּי בִי
חָשַׁק וַאֲפַלְּטֵהוּ אֲשַׂגְּבֵהוּ כִּי־יָדַע שְׁמִי: יִקְרָאֵנִי ׀
וְאֶעֱנֵהוּ עִמּוֹ אָנֹכִי בְצָרָה אֲחַלְּצֵהוּ וַאֲכַבְּדֵהוּ: אֹרֶךְ
יָמִים אַשְׂבִּיעֵהוּ וְאַרְאֵהוּ בִּישׁוּעָתִי: ארך ימים וכו'.

When the coffin is lowered into the grave, the following is to
be repeated:

עַל מְקֹמוֹ (מְקוֹמָהּ) יָבֹא (תָּבֹא) בְּשָׁלוֹם:

After the corpse is deposited in the grave, the above Psalm ישב
בסתר is repeated; after which the mourners recite the following
קדיש (Kaddish):

יִתְגַּדַּל וְיִתְקַדַּשׁ שְׁמֵהּ רַבָּא בְּעָלְמָא דִּי הוּא
עָתִיד־לְאִתְחַדָּתָא וּלְאַחֲיָאָה מֵתַיָּא: וּלְאַסָּקָא יָתְהוֹן
לְחַיֵּי עָלְמָא וּלְמִבְנֵא קַרְתָּא דִי־יְרוּשְׁלֵם וּלְשַׁכְלָלָא
הֵיכְלֵהּ בְּגַוַּהּ: וּלְמֶעְקַר פָּלְחָנָא נוּכְרָאָה מִן־אַרְעָא
וְלַאֲתָבָא פָּלְחָנָא דִי־שְׁמַיָּא לְאַתְרֵיהּ וְיַמְלִיךְ
קֻדְשָׁא בְּרִיךְ הוּא בְּמַלְכוּתֵהּ וִיקָרֵהּ:

evil shall befall thee, neither shall any plague approach thy dwelling: for He will give His angels charge concerning thee, to guard thee in all thy ways. They shall bear thee on their hands, lest thou dashest thy foot against the stones. Upon the fierce lion and adder shalt thou tread, the young lion and the dragon shalt thou trample under foot. Because he delighteth in me will I deliver him; I will exalt him because he hath known my name. When he calleth upon me I will answer him; I will be with him in distress; I will deliver him, and grant him honor. With length of days will I satisfy him, and make my salvation manifest unto him.

When the coffin is lowered into the grave, the following is to be repeated:

May [he] [she] come to [his] [her] appointed place in peace.

After the corpse is deposited in the grave, the above Psalm יושב בסתר is repeated; after which the mourners recite the following קדיש (Kaddish):

May His (God's) great name be exalted and sanctified in that world in which He is ready to renovate and to revive the dead, and to restore them to an everlasting life. Then will the city of Jerusalem be rebuilt, the temple be erected therein, the worship of idols eradicated, and the only true heavenly worship restored to its primitive dignity. Then will the Holy One (blessed be He) rule in His majestic glory.

בְּחַיֵּיכוֹן וּבְיוֹמֵיכוֹן וּבְחַיֵּי דִי־כָל־בֵּית יִשְׂרָאֵל בַּעֲגָלָא

וּבִזְמַן קָרִיב, וְאִמְרוּ אָמֵן: יְהֵא שְׁמֵהּ רַבָּא מְבָרַךְ

לְעָלַם וּלְעָלְמֵי עָלְמַיָּא: יִתְבָּרַךְ וְיִשְׁתַּבַּח וְיִתְפָּאַר

וְיִתְרוֹמַם וְיִתְנַשֵּׂא וְיִתְהַדָּר וְיִתְעַלֶּה וְיִתְהַלָּל שְׁמֵהּ

דְקוּדְשָׁא: בְּרִיךְ הוּא לְעֵלָּא מִן־כָּל־בִּרְכָתָא וְשִׁירָתָא

תֻּשְׁבְּחָתָא וְנֶחֱמָתָא דַּאֲמִירָן בְּעָלְמָא וְאִמְרוּ אָמֵן:

יְהֵא שְׁלָמָא רַבָּא מִן־שְׁמַיָּא וְחַיִּים (טוֹבִים) עָלֵינוּ

וְעַל־כָּל־יִשְׂרָאֵל וְאִמְרוּ אָמֵן:

יְהִי שֵׁם יְיָ מְבֹרָךְ מֵעַתָּה וְעַד עוֹלָם:

עֹשֶׂה שָׁלוֹם בִּמְרוֹמָיו הוּא יַעֲשֶׂה שָׁלוֹם עָלֵינוּ

וְעַל־כָּל־יִשְׂרָאֵל וְאִמְרוּ אָמֵן:

עֶזְרִי מֵעִם יְיָ עֹשֵׂה שָׁמַיִם וָאָרֶץ:

Then they say:

בִּלַּע הַמָּוֶת לָנֶצַח וּמָחָה אֲדֹנָי יְיָ דִּמְעָה מֵעַל

כָּל־פָּנִים וְחֶרְפַּת עַמּוֹ יָסִיר מֵעַל־כָּל־הָאָרֶץ כִּי יְיָ

דִּבֵּר:

As soon as the mourners come home from the burial ground they
are offered the *meal of condolence*, (סעודת הבראה) which generally consists of hard boiled eggs and bread. After having partaken of this, the following *grace after the meal*, (ברכת המזון)
is recited.

בָּרוּךְ אַתָּה יְיָ, אֱלֹהֵינוּ מֶלֶךְ הָעוֹלָם, הַזָּן אֶת־

Oh, may this happen in your life-time and in your days, and in the life-time of the whole house of Israel, speedily and without delay, and say ye,

Amen. May His omnipotent name be blessed for ever and ever throughout the world.

May His hallowed name be praised, glorified, extolled, magnified, honoured, and most excellently adored, in expression far surpassing all blessings, hymns, praises, and comforts that can be expressed in the world, and say ye, Amen.

May abundance of peace and happy life be bestowed upon us and upon all Israel, and say ye, Amen.

Blessed be the name of the Eternal, from henceforth and for evermore.

May He, who establisheth peace in His high regions, grant through His mercy peace to us and all Israel, and say ye, Amen.

My relief is from the Eternal, who made the heaven and earth.

Then they say:

Death will be destroyed for ever, and the Eternal God will wipe away tears from all faces; and the rebuke of His people shall He take away from off all the earth: for the Eternal hath spoken it.

As soon as the mourners come home from the burial ground they are offered the *meal of condolence* (סעודת הבראה), which generally consists of hard boiled eggs and bread. After having partaken of this meal the following ברכת המזון (grace after the meal) is recited:

Blessed art Thou, O Eternal, our God, King of the universe! who feedeth the whole world with His

הָעוֹלָם כֻּלּוֹ בְּטוּבוֹ בְּחֵן בְּחֶסֶד וּבְרַחֲמִים הוּא נוֹתֵן
לֶחֶם לְכָל־בָּשָׂר, כִּי לְעוֹלָם חַסְדּוֹ: וּבְטוּבוֹ הַגָּדוֹל
תָּמִיד לֹא־חָסַר לָנוּ וְאַל יֶחְסַר־לָנוּ מָזוֹן לְעוֹלָם
וָעֶד: בַּעֲבוּר שְׁמוֹ הַגָּדוֹל כִּי הוּא זָן וּמְפַרְנֵס לַכֹּל
וּמֵטִיב לַכֹּל וּמֵכִין מָזוֹן לְכָל־בְּרִיּוֹתָיו אֲשֶׁר בָּרָא.
בָּרוּךְ אַתָּה יְיָ, הַזָּן אֶת־הַכֹּל:

נוֹדֶה לְךָ יְיָ אֱלֹהֵינוּ עַל שֶׁהִנְחַלְתָּ לַאֲבוֹתֵינוּ אֶרֶץ
חֶמְדָּה טוֹבָה וּרְחָבָה וְעַל שֶׁהוֹצֵאתָנוּ יְיָ אֱלֹהֵינוּ
מֵאֶרֶץ מִצְרַיִם וּפְדִיתָנוּ מִבֵּית עֲבָדִים וְעַל־בְּרִיתְךָ
שֶׁחָתַמְתָּ בִּבְשָׂרֵנוּ וְעַל־תּוֹרָתְךָ שֶׁלִּמַּדְתָּנוּ וְעַל־
חֻקֶּיךָ שֶׁהוֹדַעְתָּנוּ וְעַל־חַיִּים חֵן וָחֶסֶד שֶׁחוֹנַנְתָּנוּ
וְעַל אֲכִילַת מָזוֹן שָׁאַתָּה זָן וּמְפַרְנֵס אוֹתָנוּ תָּמִיד
בְּכָל־יוֹם וּבְכָל־עֵת וּבְכָל־שָׁעָה:

On Hanuca they add:

עַל־הַנִּסִּים וְעַל־הַפֻּרְקָן וְעַל־הַגְּבוּרוֹת וְעַל הַתְּשׁוּעוֹת
וְעַל־הַמִּלְחָמוֹת שֶׁעָשִׂיתָ לַאֲבוֹתֵינוּ בַּיָּמִים הָהֵם בַּזְּמַן
הַזֶּה:

בִּימֵי מַתִּתְיָהוּ בֶּן־יוֹחָנָן כֹּהֵן גָּדוֹל חַשְׁמוֹנַי וּבָנָיו
כְּשֶׁעָמְדָה מַלְכוּת־יָוָן הָרְשָׁעָה עַל־עַמְּךָ יִשְׂרָאֵל לְהַשְׁכִּיחָם
תּוֹרָתֶךָ וּלְהַעֲבִירָם מֵחֻקֵּי רְצוֹנֶךָ. וְאַתָּה בְּרַחֲמֶיךָ

goodness; with grace, kindness, and compassion, He giveth food to all flesh, for His mercy endureth for ever. And through His abundant goodness, food hath not yet failed us, nor will fail us for evermore : for it is because of His own great name that He feedeth and sustaineth all and doeth good unto all, and provideth for all His creatures which He hath created. Blessed art Thou, O Eternal! who feedest all.

We give thanks unto Thee, O Eternal, our God! because Thou didst cause our ancestors to inherit the good, desirable, and ample land; and because Thou, O Eternal, our God! didst bring us forth from the land of Egypt, and didst thus redeem us from the house of bondage : and because of thy covenant which Thou didst seal in our flesh, and of the law which Thou hast taught us, and of Thy statutes which Thou hast made known unto us ; and because of the life, grace, and kindness which Thou hast mercifully bestowed upon us, and of the sustaining food wherewith Thou feedest us, and sustainest us continually, every day, at all times, and at each moment.

On Hanuca they add :

We thank Thee likewise for the miracles, the redemptions, the mighty deeds, the salvation, and triumph, which thou didst perform for our fathers, in former times, at this season.

In the days of Matathias, son of Jochanan the high priest, and his sons, when the iniquitous government of Greece rose up against Thy people Israel, to make them forget thy law, and transgress the statutes of Thy will ; Thou, in Thine abundant mercy, didst rise up for them in

הָרַבִּים עָמַדְתָּ לָהֶם בְּעֵת צָרָתָם רַבְתָּ אֶת־רִיבָם דַּנְתָּ
אֶת־דִּינָם נָקַמְתָּ אֶת־נִקְמָתָם מָסַרְתָּ גִּבּוֹרִים בְּיַד חַלָּשִׁים
וְרַבִּים בְּיַד מְעַטִּים וּטְמֵאִים בְּיַד טְהוֹרִים וּרְשָׁעִים בְּיַד
צַדִּיקִים וְזֵדִים בְּיַד עוֹסְקֵי תוֹרָתֶךָ · וּלְךָ עָשִׂיתָ שֵׁם
גָּדוֹל וְקָדוֹשׁ בְּעוֹלָמֶךָ וּלְעַמְּךָ יִשְׂרָאֵל עָשִׂיתָ תְּשׁוּעָה
גְדוֹלָה וּפֻרְקָן כְּהַיּוֹם הַזֶּה · וְאַחַר כֵּן בָּאוּ בָנֶיךָ לִדְבִיר
בֵּיתֶךָ וּפִנּוּ אֶת־הֵיכָלֶךָ וְטִהֲרוּ אֶת־מִקְדָּשֶׁךָ וְהִדְלִיקוּ
נֵרוֹת בְּחַצְרוֹת קָדְשֶׁךָ וְקָבְעוּ שְׁמוֹנַת יְמֵי חֲנֻכָּה אֵלּוּ
לְהוֹדוֹת וּלְהַלֵּל לְשִׁמְךָ הַגָּדוֹל :

וְעַל־הַכֹּל יְיָ אֱלֹהֵינוּ אֲנַחְנוּ מוֹדִים לָךְ וּמְבָרְכִים
אוֹתָךְ יִתְבָּרַךְ שִׁמְךָ בְּפִי כָל־חַי תָּמִיד לְעוֹלָם וָעֶד :
כַּכָּתוּב, וְאָכַלְתָּ וְשָׂבָעְתָּ וּבֵרַכְתָּ אֶת־יְיָ אֱלֹהֶיךָ עַל־
הָאָרֶץ הַטֹּבָה אֲשֶׁר נָתַן־לָךְ · בָּרוּךְ אַתָּה יְיָ, עַל־
הָאָרֶץ וְעַל־הַמָּזוֹן :

רַחֵם יְיָ אֱלֹהֵינוּ עַל־יִשְׂרָאֵל עַמֶּךָ וְעַל־יְרוּשָׁלַיִם
עִירֶךָ וְעַל־צִיּוֹן מִשְׁכַּן כְּבוֹדֶךָ וְעַל־מַלְכוּת בֵּית דָּוִד
מְשִׁיחֶךָ וְעַל־הַבַּיִת הַגָּדוֹל וְהַקָּדוֹשׁ שֶׁנִּקְרָא שִׁמְךָ
עָלָיו : אֱלֹהֵינוּ אָבִינוּ רְעֵנוּ זוּנֵנוּ פַּרְנְסֵנוּ וְכַלְכְּלֵנוּ
וְהַרְוִיחֵנוּ וְהַרְוַח־לָנוּ יְיָ אֱלֹהֵינוּ מְהֵרָה מִכָּל־
צָרוֹתֵינוּ : וְנָא אַל־תַּצְרִיכֵנוּ יְיָ אֱלֹהֵינוּ לֹא לִידֵי

the time of their trouble, didst contend for their cause, didst judge their suit, and avenge their wrongs. Thou didst deliver the mighty into the hands of the weak ; the multitude into the hands of the few ; the impure into the hands of the undefiled ; the wicked into the hands of the righteous, and the proud into the hands of those who engage in the study of Thy law. Thus didst Thou make unto Thyself a great and holy name in Thy world; and didst work a great salvation and redemption for Thy people Israel as at this day: After this Thy children entered into the oracle of Thine house, cleansed Thy temple, purified Thy holy place, and rekindled the lights in the courts of Thy holy house: and they appointed these eight days of dedication to be celebrated with thanksgiving and praise to Thy great name.

And for all these things, O Eternal, our God! we give thanks unto Thee, and bless Thee. Blessed shall Thy name continually be in the mouth of every living being for ever and ever, as it is written, "When thou hast eaten, and art satisfied, thou shalt bless the Eternal, thy God, for the goodly land which He hath given unto thee." Blessed art Thou, O Eternal! for the land and for the food.

Have compassion, we beseech Thee, O Eternal, our God! on Thy people Israel, upon Jerusalem Thy city, on Zion the residence of Thy glory, on the kingdom of the house of David, Thine anointed, and on the great and holy house which is called by Thy name. O our God, our Father! feed, sustain, support, and maintain us, and grant us enlargement. Enlarge us speedily, O Eternal, our God! from all our troubles; and let us not, we pray Thee, O Eternal, our God !

מַתְּנַת בָּשָׂר וָדָם וְלֹא לִידֵי הַלְוָאָתָם כִּי אִם־לְיָדְךָ
הַמְּלֵאָה הַפְּתוּחָה הַקְּדוֹשָׁה וְהָרְחָבָה שֶׁלֹּא נֵבוֹשׁ
וְלֹא נִכָּלֵם לְעוֹלָם וָעֶד:

On Sabbath add:

רְצֵה וְהַחֲלִיצֵנוּ יְיָ אֱלֹהֵינוּ בְּמִצְוֹתֶיךָ וּבְמִצְוַת יוֹם
הַשְּׁבִיעִי הַשַּׁבָּת וְהַגָּדוֹל וְהַקָּדוֹשׁ הַזֶּה כִּי יוֹם זֶה גָּדוֹל
וְקָדוֹשׁ הוּא לְפָנֶיךָ לִשְׁבָּת־בּוֹ וְלָנוּחַ בּוֹ בְּאַהֲבָה
כְּמִצְוַת רְצוֹנֶךָ: בִּרְצוֹנְךָ הָנִיחַ לָנוּ יְיָ אֱלֹהֵינוּ שֶׁלֹּא
תְהִי צָרָה וְיָגוֹן וַאֲנָחָה בְּיוֹם מְנוּחָתֵנוּ. וְהַרְאֵנוּ יְיָ
אֱלֹהֵינוּ בְּנֶחָמַת צִיּוֹן עִירֶךָ וּבְבִנְיַן יְרוּשָׁלַיִם עִיר קָדְשֶׁךָ
כִּי אַתָּה הוּא בַּעַל הַיְשׁוּעוֹת וּבַעַל הַנֶּחָמוֹת:

On New Moon add:

אֱלֹהֵינוּ וֵאלֹהֵי אֲבוֹתֵינוּ. יַעֲלֶה וְיָבֹא וְיַגִּיעַ וְיֵרָאֶה
וְיֵרָצֶה וְיִשָּׁמַע וְיִפָּקֵד וְיִזָּכֵר זִכְרוֹנֵנוּ וּפִקְדוֹנֵנוּ וְזִכְרוֹן
אֲבוֹתֵינוּ. וְזִכְרוֹן מָשִׁיחַ בֶּן־דָּוִד עַבְדֶּךָ. וְזִכְרוֹן
יְרוּשָׁלַיִם עִיר קָדְשֶׁךָ. וְזִכְרוֹן כָּל־עַמְּךָ בֵּית יִשְׂרָאֵל
לְפָנֶיךָ לִפְלֵיטָה וּלְטוֹבָה וּלְחֵן וּלְחֶסֶד וּלְרַחֲמִים וּלְחַיִּים
וּלְשָׁלוֹם בְּיוֹם רֹאשׁ הַחֹדֶשׁ הַזֶּה: זָכְרֵנוּ יְיָ אֱלֹהֵינוּ בּוֹ
לְטוֹבָה, וּפָקְדֵנוּ בוֹ לִבְרָכָה, וְהוֹשִׁיעֵנוּ בוֹ לְחַיִּים.
וּבִדְבַר יְשׁוּעָה וְרַחֲמִים חוּס וְחָנֵּנוּ. וְרַחֵם עָלֵינוּ
וְהוֹשִׁיעֵנוּ. כִּי אֵלֶיךָ עֵינֵינוּ. כִּי אֵל (מֶלֶךְ) חַנּוּן וְרַחוּם
אָתָּה:

stand in need, either of the gifts of mankind, or of loans; but let us depend only on Thy hand which is ever full, open, holy, and liberal, so that we may never be put to shame nor confounded.

On Sabbath add:

Be pleased, O Eternal, our God! to felicitate us through Thy commandments, and especially through the commandment of the seventh day, — this great and holy Sabbath; for this day is great and holy in Thy presence, that we may rest thereon, and to be at repose thereon, in pious love, according to the command of Thy will. In Thy favour, O Eternal, our God! grant us repose, that there be no trouble, sorrow or sighing, to afflict us on our day of rest; but cause us to behold, O Eternal, our God, the consolation of Zion, Thy city, and the rebuilding of Jerusalem, Thy holy city; for Thou art He who is the Lord of salvation, and the Lord of consolation.

On New Moon add:

Our God, and the God of our Fathers! suffer to ascend, arrive, approach, appear, and be accepted; to be heard, borne in mind, and remembered before Thee, our memorial, and the memorial of our fathers, the memorial of the Messiah, the son of David Thy servant, the memorial of Jerusalem, Thy holy city, and the memorial of all Thy people the house of Israel, to obtain for us deliverance, happiness, grace, favour, and compassion, life and peace, on this first day of the month. O Eternal, our God, remember us thereon for good, and visit us thereon with a blessing, and save us thereon, to enjoy life. And with the word of salvation and mercy, have pity, and be gracious unto us. O have compassion upon us, and save us, for our eyes are towards thee, because thou, O God! art a merciful and compassionate King!

נַחֵם יְיָ אֱלֹהֵינוּ אֶת־אֲבֵלֵי יְרוּשָׁלַיִם וְאֶת־הָאֲבֵלִים
הַמִּתְאַבְּלִים בָּאֵבֶל הַזֶּה, נַחֲמֵם מֵאָבְלָם וְשַׂמְּחֵם
מִיגוֹנָם, כָּאָמוּר כְּאִישׁ אֲשֶׁר אִמּוֹ תְּנַחֲמֶנּוּ כֵּן אָנֹכִי
אֲנַחֶמְכֶם וּבִירוּשָׁלַיִם תְּנֻחָמוּ, בָּרוּךְ אַתָּה יְיָ מְנַחֵם
צִיּוֹן בְּבִנְיַן יְרוּשָׁלָיִם:

בָּרוּךְ אַתָּה יְיָ, אֱלֹהֵינוּ מֶלֶךְ הָעוֹלָם, הָאֵל אָבִינוּ
מַלְכֵּנוּ, בּוֹרְאֵנוּ גֹּאֲלֵנוּ קְדוֹשֵׁנוּ קְדוֹשׁ יַעֲקֹב, הַמֶּלֶךְ
הַחַי, הַטּוֹב וְהַמֵּטִיב, אֵל אֱמֶת, דַּיָן אֱמֶת, שׁוֹפֵט
צֶדֶק, (וְלֹקֵחַ נְפָשׁוֹת בְּמִשְׁפָּט), וְשַׁלִּיט בְּעוֹלָמוֹ
לַעֲשׂוֹת בּוֹ כִּרְצוֹנוֹ, כִּי כָל־דְּרָכָיו מִשְׁפָּט, וַאֲנַחְנוּ
עַמּוֹ וַעֲבָדָיו: וְעַל־הַכֹּל אֲנַחְנוּ חַיָּבִים לְהוֹדוֹת לוֹ
וּלְבָרְכוֹ. גֹּדֵר פִּרְצוֹת יִשְׂרָאֵל הוּא יִגְדֹּר אֶת־הַפִּרְצָה
הַזֹּאת מֵעָלֵינוּ (וּמֵעַל הָאָבֵל הַזֶּה) לְחַיִּים וּלְשָׁלוֹם,
הוּא יִגְמְלֵנוּ לָעַד חֵן וָחֶסֶד וְרַחֲמִים וְכָל־טוֹב, וּמִכָּל־
טוֹב אַל יְחַסְּרֵנוּ:

הָרַחֲמָן הוּא יִמְלוֹךְ עָלֵינוּ לְעוֹלָם וָעֶד: הָרַחֲמָן
הוּא יִתְבָּרַךְ בַּשָּׁמַיִם וּבָאָרֶץ: הָרַחֲמָן הוּא יִשְׁתַּבַּח
לְדוֹר דּוֹרִים וְיִתְפָּאַר בָּנוּ לָנֶצַח נְצָחִים וְיִתְהַדַּר
בָּנוּ לָעַד וּלְעוֹלְמֵי עוֹלָמִים: הָרַחֲמָן הוּא יְפַרְנְסֵנוּ

Console, O Lord, our God, the mourners of Jerusalem and the mourners in this place. Give them consolation in their bereavement and grant them strength
in their affliction. As it is written: like the man com-
forted by his mother, thus I shall comfort you, and
in Jerusalem ye will be consoled. Blessed art Thou,
O Eternal, Comforter of Zion and Jerusalem.

Blessed art Thou, O Eternal, our God, King of the
universe, Omnipotent! our Father, our King, our
Strength, our Creator, our Redeemer, our Holy One,
the Holy One of Jacob, our Shepherd, the Shepherd of Israel, the eternally living King, who
is good and beneficent, the God of truth, who
judgeth with righteousness; who in judgment re-
calleth the souls of His children, who ruleth over His
world to execute His will; all of whose ways are just
towards us who are His people and His servants.
And for all these things we are bound to give thanks
unto Him, and to bless Him who repaireth the
breaches of Israel. May He repair this breach for
us, and for all His people of the house of Israel unto
life and peace; He will deal bountifully with us,
granting us grace, favour and every good; yea, of no
good will He cause us to be deficient.

May the All-merciful reign over us for ever and
ever! May the All-merciful be praised in heaven and
earth! May the All-merciful be praised throughout all
generations, be glorified among us to everlasting, and
be honoured in our midst, for ever and to all eternity!
May the All-merciful sustain us with honour! May

בִּכְבוֹד: הָרַחֲמָן, הוּא יִשְׁבּוֹר עֻלֵנוּ מֵעַל צַוָּארֵנוּ

וְהוּא יוֹלִיכֵנוּ קוֹמְמִיּוּת לְאַרְצֵנוּ: הָרַחֲמָן, הוּא

יִשְׁלַח בְּרָכָה מְרֻבָּה בַּבַּיִת הַזֶּה וְעַל־שֻׁלְחָן זֶה

שֶׁאָכַלְנוּ עָלָיו: הָרַחֲמָן, הוּא יִשְׁלַח לָנוּ אֶת־אֵלִיָּה

הַנָּבִיא זָכוּר לַטּוֹב וִיבַשֶּׂר־לָנוּ בְּשׂוֹרוֹת טוֹבוֹת

יְשׁוּעוֹת וְנֶחָמוֹת: הָרַחֲמָן, הוּא יְבָרֵךְ אֶת (אָבִי)

מוֹרִי בַּעַל הַבַּיִת הַזֶּה וְאֶת (אִמִּי) מוֹרָתִי בַּעֲלַת

הַבַּיִת הַזֶּה אוֹתָם וְאֶת־בֵּיתָם וְאֶת־זַרְעָם וְאֶת־כָּל־

אֲשֶׁר־לָהֶם אוֹתָנוּ וְאֶת־כָּל־אֲשֶׁר־לָנוּ. כְּמוֹ שֶׁנִּתְבָּרְכוּ

אֲבוֹתֵינוּ אַבְרָהָם יִצְחָק וְיַעֲקֹב בַּכֹּל מִכֹּל כֹּל, כֵּן

יְבָרֵךְ אוֹתָנוּ כֻּלָּנוּ יַחַד בִּבְרָכָה שְׁלֵמָה, וְנֹאמַר אָמֵן:

בַּמָּרוֹם יְלַמְּדוּ עֲלֵיהֶם וְעָלֵינוּ זְכוּת שֶׁתְּהִי לְמִשְׁמֶרֶת

שָׁלוֹם. וְנִשָּׂא בְרָכָה מֵאֵת יְיָ וּצְדָקָה מֵאֱלֹהֵי

יִשְׁעֵנוּ, וְנִמְצָא־חֵן וְשֵׂכֶל טוֹב בְּעֵינֵי אֱלֹהִים וְאָדָם:

לשבת

הָרַחֲמָן, הוּא יַנְחִילֵנוּ יוֹם שֶׁכֻּלּוֹ שַׁבָּת וּמְנוּחָה לְחַיֵּי

הָעוֹלָמִים:

לראש חדש

הָרַחֲמָן, הוּא יְחַדֵּשׁ עָלֵינוּ אֶת־הַחוֹדֶשׁ הַזֶּה לְטוֹבָה

וְלִבְרָכָה:

the All-merciful break the yoke of captivity from off our neck, and lead us in security to our land! May the All-merciful send us abundant blessing on this house, and on this table at which we have eaten! May the All-merciful send us Elijah the prophet (of happy memory) that he may announce to us tidings of happines, salvation, and consolation! May the All-merciful bless [my father* and instructor] the master of this house, and [my mother and instructress] the mistress of this house, and with them, their household, their children, and all that belongs to them; us, and all that belongs to us; even as our ancestors Abraham, Isaac, and Jacob were severally blessed in all things, through all things and with all things; thus may he bless us, even all of us altogether, with a complete blessing, and let us say, Amen.

In the high heaven may they obtain for them and for us the felicity of the Divine guardianship over our welfare that we may receive a blessing from the Eternal and righteousness from the God of our salvation, and that we may find grace and due regard in the eyes of God and man.

On Sabbath say:

May the All-merciful cause us to inherit the day that is all Sabbath and repose in eternal life.

On New Moon say:

May the All-merciful renew this month for us as a benefit and a blessing.

---

* The names in this verse, within brackets, are omitted if the parents should not be present, and other names substituted in their stead.

הָרַחֲמָן הוּא יְזַכֵּנוּ לִימוֹת הַמָּשִׁיחַ וּלְחַיֵּי הָעוֹלָם
הַבָּא: מַגְדִּיל (נראש חדש ובשבת אומרים מִגְדּוֹל) יְשׁוּעוֹת
מַלְכּוֹ וְעֹשֶׂה חֶסֶד לִמְשִׁיחוֹ לְדָוִד וּלְזַרְעוֹ עַד־עוֹלָם:
עֹשֶׂה שָׁלוֹם בִּמְרוֹמָיו הוּא יַעֲשֶׂה שָׁלוֹם עָלֵינוּ וְעַל
כָּל־יִשְׂרָאֵל, וְאִמְרוּ אָמֵן:

יְראוּ אֶת־יְיָ קְדֹשָׁיו כִּי אֵין מַחְסוֹר לִירֵאָיו:
כְּפִירִים רָשׁוּ וְרָעֵבוּ וְדֹרְשֵׁי יְיָ לֹא־יַחְסְרוּ כָל־טוֹב:
הוֹדוּ לַיְיָ כִּי־טוֹב כִּי לְעוֹלָם חַסְדּוֹ: פּוֹתֵחַ אֶת־יָדֶךָ
וּמַשְׂבִּיעַ לְכָל־חַי רָצוֹן: בָּרוּךְ הַגֶּבֶר אֲשֶׁר יִבְטַח
בַּיְיָ וְהָיָה יְיָ מִבְטַחוֹ:

נַעַר הָיִיתִי גַּם זָקַנְתִּי וְלֹא־רָאִיתִי צַדִּיק נֶעֱזָב
וְזַרְעוֹ מְבַקֶּשׁ לָחֶם:

יְיָ עֹז לְעַמּוֹ יִתֵּן, יְיָ ׀ יְבָרֵךְ אֶת־עַמּוֹ בַשָּׁלוֹם:

In the house of mourning the Mincha [מנחה] and Maarib [מעריב]
prayers are said.

May the All-merciful render us worthy to behold the days of Messiah, and of the eternal life in a future state. He giveth great (*On Sabbath and New Moons say:* He is a tower of) salvation to His king and acteth mercifully towards his anointed, towards David and his progeny for ever. May He who maketh peace in His high heavens, in His mercy, grant peace unto us and unto all Israel, and say ye, Amen.

Fear the Eternal, ye His holy ones, for no want have those who fear Him. Even young lions lack and suffer hunger; but they who seek the Eternal shall not lack any good. Give thanks unto the Eternal, for He is good, for His mercy endureth for ever. Thou openest Thine hand, and satisfiest the desire of every living being. Blessed is the man who trusteth in the Eternal, for the Eternal will be his protection.

I have been young, and am now old, yet never did I see the righteous entirely forsaken, nor his offspring begging bread.

The Eternal will give strength to His people: the Eternal will bless His people with peace.

———

In the house of mourning the Mincha [מנחה] and Maarib [מעריב] prayers are said.

———

After the Maarib prayer the following Psalm is said, after which קדיש is recited.

מִכְתָּם לְדָוִד שָׁמְרֵנִי אֵל כִּי־חָסִיתִי בָךְ׃ אָמַרְתְּ

לַיהוָה אֲדֹנָי אָתָּה טוֹבָתִי בַּל־עָלֶיךָ׃ לִקְדוֹשִׁים

אֲשֶׁר־בָּאָרֶץ הֵמָּה וְאַדִּירֵי כָּל־חֶפְצִי־בָם׃ יִרְבּוּ

עַצְּבוֹתָם אַחֵר מָהָרוּ בַּל־אַסִּיךְ נִסְכֵּיהֶם מִדָּם וּבַל־

אֶשָּׂא אֶת־שְׁמוֹתָם עַל־שְׂפָתָי׃ יְהוָה מְנָת חֶלְקִי

וְכוֹסִי אַתָּה תּוֹמִיךְ גּוֹרָלִי׃ חֲבָלִים נָפְלוּ־לִי בַּנְּעִמִים

אַף־נַחֲלָת שָׁפְרָה עָלָי׃ אֲבָרֵךְ אֶת־יְהוָה אֲשֶׁר

יְעָצָנִי אַף־לֵילוֹת יִסְּרוּנִי כִלְיוֹתָי׃ שִׁוִּיתִי יְהוָה

לְנֶגְדִּי תָמִיד כִּי מִימִינִי בַּל־אֶמּוֹט׃ לָכֵן ׀ שָׂמַח לִבִּי

וַיָּגֶל כְּבוֹדִי אַף־בְּשָׂרִי יִשְׁכֹּן לָבֶטַח׃ כִּי ׀ לֹא־תַעֲזֹב

נַפְשִׁי לִשְׁאוֹל לֹא־תִתֵּן חֲסִידְךָ לִרְאוֹת שָׁחַת׃

תּוֹדִיעֵנִי אֹרַח חַיִּים שֹׂבַע שְׂמָחוֹת אֶת־פָּנֶיךָ נְעִמוֹת

בִּימִינְךָ נֶצַח׃   קדיש יתום.

After the Maarib prayer the following Psalm is said; after which
the קדיש is recited.

MICHTAM OF DAVID.

Protect me, O God! for in Thee do I put my
trust, O my felicity. Say thou unto the Eternal,
Thou art my Lord : nought excelleth Thee. *Say it
also* to the holy in the land, and to the mighty nobles
in whom are all my delights. Their sorrows increase
who follow strange gods: I will not offer their liba-
tions of blood, neither will I utter their names with
my lips. Thou, O Eternal, art the portion of mine
inheritance and of my cup. Thou maintainest my
lot. My portion was assigned to me in pleasantness; yea, mine is a goodly heritage. *Now* will I
praise the Eternal, who thus gave me counsel; even
in *dismal* nights, in inward chastisements, have I set
the Eternal always before me, He is at my right
hand, I shall not be shaken. Therefore my heart
is glad, and my glory rejoiceth; even my flesh shall
also rest in peace. For Thou wilt not doom my soul
to perdition; neither wilt Thou suffer Thy pious
ones to see corruption. Thou wilt show me the path
of life; in Thy presence is fulness of joy, at Thy
right hand everlasting beatitude.

After the recitation of the Psalm and the Kaddish for the orphans, one of the following seven portions of the Talmud, arranged for the שבעה, is to be read by the minister or some other person.

1. הנו רבנן. מעשה במונבז המלך. שבזבז אוצרותיו ואוצרות
אבותיו . בשנת בצורת . וחברו עליו אחיו יבית אביו . ואמרו לו :
אבותיך גנזו אוצרות והוסיפו על של אבותיו . ואתה מבזבז אוצרותיך
ואוצרות אבותיך . אמר להם : אבותי גנזו למטה ואני גנזתי למעלה :
שנאמר אמת מארץ תצמח וצדק משמים נשקף : אבותי גנזו במקום
שהיד שולטת בהם. ואני גנזתי במקום שאין היד שולטת בהם:
שנאמר צדק ומשפט מכון כסאך : אבותי גנזו דבר שאין עושה

Our Sages relate:—During the reign of King Mo-nobazus, there happened to be a most grievous famine. The humane king, moved by the sufferings and privations of his people, caused the treasures, which he and his ancestors had amassed, to be distributed amongst the poor and needy. He was severely reproached by his brethren, and by all his family. Thy forefathers, said they, hoarded up treasures, and augmented those of thy ancestors, but thou, so far from increasing them, dost even squander what they have left. The benevolent king replied, My fathers have gathered terrestrial treasures, I have saved celestial ones. As Scripture says: "Truth must spring forth out of the earth, then benevolence will look down from heaven." My fathers hid treasures within the reach of ruthless hands, mine are preserved in a place beyond the reach of human violence. As it is said, "Justice and judgment are the basis of Thy throne, when mercy and truth anticipate Thy presence." My fathers garnered that which yields no fruit, that

פירות׳ ואני ננזתי דבר שעושה פירות: שנאמר אמרו צדיק כי טוב.
כי פרי מעלליהם יאכלו: אבותי גנזו אוצרות ממון. ואני גנזתי
אוצרות נפשות. שנאמר ולוקח נפשות חכם: אבותי גנזו לאחרים.
ואני גנזתי לעצמי. שנאמר ולך תהיה צדקה: אבותי גנזו לעולם׳
הזה. ואני גנזתי לעולם הבא: שנאמר והלך לפניך צדקך כבוד
ה׳ יאספך:

_____

2. תניא. היה רבי מאיר אומר. טוב ללכת אל בית אבל.
מלכת אל בית המשתה. כאשר הוא סוף כל האדם. והחי יתן

_____

which I have preserved will produce fruit in abundance. As Scripture says: "Say ye to the righteous that it shall be well with them; for they shall
eat the fruit of their doings," My fathers, indeed,
have preserved gold, I have saved souls; as Scripture says: "And he that winneth souls is wise."
My fathers have amassed for others, what I amass
is for myself; as we read: "And it shall be righteousness unto THEE before the Eternal thy God."
In a word, my fore-fathers have amassed stores for
this world, I, on the contrary, have saved for that
to come; as Scripture says: "Thy righteousness
shall precede thee; the glory of the Eternal shall
be thy reward."

_____

Rabbi Meyer thus comments on the following
Scriptural passage: "It is better to go to the house
of mourning than to go to the house of feasting; for
that is the end of all men, and the living will lay it

אל לבו. מאי והחי יתן אל לבו: דברים של מיתה. דיספד
יספדוניה. דיקבר יקברוניה. דיטען יטעוניה. דילווה ילוויה. דידל
ידלוניה. כדאיתא במ"ק פרק ג': כי מידותיו של הקב"ה. מדה
כנגד מדה: וההולך לנחם האבלים. הקב"ה בעצמו ינחמו. על
כן ילך האדם לקיים המצוה הגדולה. לנחם האבלים העצומים
בינון ואנחה. וידבר אל לבם דברי נחומין. ובזה גומל הסד. ועשה
מדה הקב"ה. כי הוא בעצמו ניחם את יצחק. דכתיב ויהי אחרי
מות אברהם. ויברך אלהים את יצחק בנו. שנחמו תנחומי אבלים:
וכן אליהו הנביא. שהלך לנחם את היאל. בית האלי. ואהאב שהיה

to his heart." What, asks the Rabbi, is man to
take to his heart? To be at all times conscious
of his own frailty, and not to forget the awful
truth that he likewise will once stand in need of
the same service he now renders to the dead. As
he mourns for others, thus others will mourn for
him ; as he buries others, as he carries and follows
others to their resting-place, the same will others do
to him. For the same measure we mete out to
others, the Eternal will mete out to us. And he
who comforts the mourners will, when in distress,
find consolation in God. Son of man, fulfil, therefore,
this charitable and humane duty, visit and console
the distressed mourners, soothe their grief, cheer
them, speak to them words of comfort and consolation, and thou wilt follow thy Creator, who consoled
our patriarch Isaac in time of grief; as we read:
"And it came to pass after the death of Abraham,
and God blessed his son Isaac ; which our sages
illustrate, God spoke to his heart words of comfort.
Tradition tells that Elijah went to condole Hiel, the
Beth-elite, who, when rebuilding the city of Jericho,

רשע. והיה מלך. אף על פי כן הלך לנחם את היאל בית האלי.
כשמתו בניו משום שבנה העיר יריחו: ובזה עושה נחת רוח
להיים ולמהים. וגם הוא עצמו על ידי זה נותן אל לבו דברים
של מיתה. ולשוב מחטאיו:

---

3. הבא לנחם אבלים. יאמר להם דברים של טעם בנחמתו
כדי שיצדיקו דינם. ויקבלו התנחומים: כמו שאמר דוד. בעוד

---

had lost his two sons, as enunciated by Joshuah. And
king Ahab, ungodly as he was, still condescended
personally to condole the bereaved father in his
affliction. These events fully demonstrate the importance of comforting the mourners.

He who is solicitous of performing the duty of
condoling the mourners, not as a mere outward
ceremony, but in the true sense of its sacred institu-
tion, should address the mourners in words of comfort, reasonable and pious observations, so as to
induce them, however grievously afflicted by their
recent loss, to acknowledge the justice of God, who
alone can afford salvation. The demeanor of king
David, on the occasion of the death of his child, as
narrated in Holy Writ, is at once so instructive and
consoling that we deem it proper to quote it at
length. A child, of which this pious king was ex-
tremely fond, and whom he so paternally loved, was
overtaken with a dangerous illness. "David, therefore," says Scripture, "besought God for the child.
And David fasted, and went in, and lay all night
upon the earth ; and the elders of his house arose,

הילד חי צמתי ואבכה כי אמרתי. מי יודע וחנני ה". וחי הילד:
ועתה מת. למה זה אני צם. האוכל להשיבו עוד. אני הלך אליו
והוא לא ישוב אלי:

---

and went to him to raise him up from the earth: but
he would not, neither did he eat bread with them.
And it came to pass on the seventh day, that the
child died. And the servants of David feared to
tell him that the child was dead; for, said they,
behold while the child was yet alive, we spake unto
him, and he would not hearken unto our voice, how
will he then vex himself, if we tell him the child is
dead? But when David saw that his servants whis-
pered, David perceived that the child was dead;
therefore he said to his servants: is the child dead?
and they said: it is dead. Then David rose from
the earth, and washed and anointed himself, and
changed his apparel, and came into the house of the
Eternal and worshipped, and then he came into his
own house; and when he required they set bread
before him, and he did eat. Then said his servants
unto him: what thing is this that thou hast done?
Thou didst fast and weep for the child when the
child was alive; but when the child was dead, thou
didst rise and eat bread. And he said: while the
child was yet alive, I fasted and wept; for I said:
who can tell whether God will be gracious to me,
that the child may live? but now it is dead, wherefore should I fast? Can I bring him back? I shall
go to him, but he will not return to me."

כי כל מה שיכסה העפר.

יכסה מן הבשר:

כי הם למנוחה.

ואנחנו ביגון ואנחה:

על כן אין להתרעם אחר מדותיו. כי צדיק וישר הוא. ומי
יאמר לו מה העשה: ואין לנו רק להצדיק דינו על כל מה שעשה:
ה" נתן וה" לקח יהי שם ה" מבורך: ומי שיבכה על מת יותר
מדאי. כאילו מתרעם על מדות הקב"ה:

‎4. אמר רב יהודא אמר רב כל המתקשה על מתו יותר
מדאי. על מת אחר הוא בוכה. כי הא דרב הונא. הוי הך

Wise Providence ordained that whatever earth
covers, man forgets; for—

Why should we grieve and mourn for those
Who have gone to their everlasting repose?

Let us, therefore, refrain from complaining against
the ways of God; for He is just and upright, and
who can say unto Him: what doest Thou? On the
contrary, we have but to acknowledge the equity of
His judgment in all His proceedings towards us.
"The Eternal hath given, and the Eternal hath taken
away; blessed be the name of God!" By excessive
lamentation, by unremitting weeping for the dead,
we manifest that we are discontent with the dispensation of His Divine justice.

Rabbi Jehudah says in the name of Rav: he who
frets or gives way to excessive grief at the death of
a relative or friend, will have cause to bewail the
loss of another dear and beloved individual.

אתתא בשיבבותיה. דהוו לה שבע בנין. שכיב חד מינייהו. הוות
בכיא עליה טובה. אמר לה רב הונא לא העבוד הכי. ולא
אשגחית ביה. שלח לה. אי ציית מוטב: ואם לאו תכניש ההיא
איתתא. זודתא לאידך. ומיתי כלהון. כדמייהו כולהון. אמר תכנוש
זוודתא לנפשה ומתה: אל תבכו למת. ולא הנודו לו. אל תבכו
למת. יותר מדאי. ואל תנודו לו. יותר מכשיעור. אלא שלשה
לבכי. שבעה להספד. שלשים להספורה. מכאן ואילך אמר הקב"ה

Near the residence of Rabbi Hunah, there lived a
woman who had lost one of her seven sons, at which
calamity she fretted and wept so grievously, that
Rabbi Hunah was induced to request her to cease
from such impious lamentation. She, however, turned
a deaf ear to the friendly words of the pious Rabbi.
He again said unto her: "if thou wilt follow my ad-
vice, it will be well unto thee; if not, thou mayest
prepare shrouds for another of thy sons." These
well-meant words, however, had no effect upon her;
she still continued to give vent to her violent complaints, until she was bereaved of all her children·
Rabbi Hunah again entreated her to submit to the
will of God, and consider her own life; but, alas,
even these admonishing words had no influence upon
her, and ultimately she herself fell a victim to her
excessive fretting. The passage in Jeremiah: "weep
ye not for the dead, neither bemoan him," is thus ex-
pounded by the Talmud: "weep not for the dead to
excess, and bemoan him not more than the duty of
nature demands. Three days ought to be devoted
to weeping, seven days to mourning, and thirty days
for the growing of the hair.* But by lamenting

* To abstain from cutting the hair of the head and beard.

אין אתם מרחמים עליו יותר ממני: ואמר רב יהודה. מה שאין
לו מנהמין. הולכין עשרה בני אדם ויושבין במקומו: ההוא דשכיב
בשיבבותיה דרב יהודה. ולא הוה ליה מנהמין. כל יומא מדבר
רב יהודה עשרה. ויהבי בדוכתיה. אהחזי ליה בחלמא. ואמר ליה.
תנוח דעתך. שהנחת את דעתי: ונמצא שמצוה גדולה ליכנוס
עשרה בני אדם כל שבעה. ולהתפלל שם. וללמוד אחר
התפלה. אפילו במח קטן. מכל שכן במה גדול וביותר שיש לו

beyond this time we incur the just reproach of Almighty God, whose voice, as it were, calls upon us:
'son of man, hast thou more compassion upon the
departed than I, the merciful God?'" The same
Rabbi also recommends as a praisworthy custom,
viz.: at the demise of a person who left no relatives
to mourn for him, to send, during the seven days of
mourning, ten men to the house where his death
took place, there to perform the daily service. A
death happened near the residence of Rahbi Jehudah, and there were no relatives to mourn for the
deceased; in consequence of which Rabbi Jehudah
brought to the house of the departed ten men, who
joined him in prayer, which so greatly absorbed the
thoughts of the truly humane Rabbi, that he dreamt
to have seen the departed, who said to him: "mayest
thou enjoy the same repose and spiritual tranquility
which thou hast caused to be conferred upon me."
Hence we perceive the importance of the pious and
humane duties, as instituted by our sages, during
the שבעה (the seven days); there to pray, and there
to meditate on the law of God. These duties must
be observed even at the death of a child. And in
case the deceased left a son, care should be taken

בן. שיאמר קדיש על אביו ואמו. שמצילם מן הגיהנם ומעלה
אותם לגן ערן: ומה טוב ונעים שילמדו שם עשרה חבמים כל
השנה ראשונה. שעה אחת. בכל יום בעבור המת. כדי שיאמר
כל פעם קדיש דרבנן: ועל כל פנים ימי השלשים:

----

5. תנו רבנן שלשה שותפין באדם, הקב"ה ואביו ואמו, הם
נותנין הזרע, שממנה נוצר הגוף, שהוא בשר ודם; והקב"ה נותן
בו קלסתר פניו, וראיות עין, ושמיעת אזן, ודבור פה, והילוך רגלים,

----

that he say קדיש for his departed father or mother,
and to implore God that He may redeem them from
the גיהנם, and place them in the garden of Eden.
The sages also recommend as a praiseworthy ob-
servance on the mournful occasion of death, that
ten pious men, who are versed in the Law of God,
should daily assemble for an hour at least during the
first year of mourning, at the house of the departed;
there to pray, meditate and study the Law of God;
at the conclusion of which the well-known קדיש דרבן
is to be recited. Should, however, circumstances
not permit us to observe these customs through the
whole year, they ought at least not be neglected
during the thirty days subsequent to the death.

The Rabbis observe: man owes his existence first
to God, and then to his father and mother. To the
latter he owes the physical life, whilst the Omnipotent invests him with 'form and features, faculties
and intellect, which distinguish him from the animal
creation. Through Him the eye seeth, and the ear
heareth; through Him the mouth speaketh, and the

ודעה ובינה ושכל: וכיון שהגיע זמנו לפטר מן העולם, הקב"ה
נוטל חלקו, והלק אביו ואמו מונח לפניהם: אמר רב פפא היינו
דאמרי אינשא: פוץ מלחא ושדי בשרא לכלבא כדאיתא בקדושין
פ"א: וכן אמר דוד, אבי ואמי יעזבני וה" יאספני: שהם עושין
כשביל הנאתן, ואחר כך זה פונה לכאן וזו פונה לכאן והקב"ה
צייר הטפה ונוצר ממנה האדם:

ובן אמר איוב: הלא כחלב התיכני וכגבינה הקפיאני עור
ובשר הלבישני וגו" חיים והסד עשית עמדי וגו": ועל כן כתיב
מי חכם וישמר אלה ויתבוננו חסדי ה": על כן מי האיש החפץ
חיים, חיי עולם הבא, יבין בחסדי ה" ויגמול גם הוא הסד ואמת:

---

foot walketh. From Him are knowledge, discernment and understanding. When the hour of death approacheth, the Almighty claims His portion, and leaves to father and mother their own share . . .

Thus saith Job: "Hast Thou not poured me out as milk, and curdled me as cheese? Thou hast clothed me with skin and flesh, and hast formed me with bones and sinews. Thou hast granted me life and favor, and Thy visitation hath preserved my spirit." How just, therefore, is the exhortation of king David, in exclaiming: "whoso is wise will observe these things, even they shall understand the loving kindnesses of the Eternal." How diligently ought he, who desireth life everlasting, contemplate the mercies of God, in order that he may emulate them; that he, like God, may disinterestedly exercise benevolence and unselfish charity in supporting the living, and not relax or shrink back from participating in the duties which we owe to the mortal remains of our fellow creatures.

6. אמר שלמה המלך: הכל הולך אל מקום אחד. הכל
היה מן העפר והכל שב אל העפר: כמות זה כן מות זה:
מותא כמותא ומרעא חיבוליא: הנה אשרי אנוש יוכיחנו אלוה
ומוסר שדי אל תמאס: כי הוא יכאיב ויחבש יכהץ וידיו תרפינה:
כי היסורין הם לטובת האדם ובהסד. לפי כח האדם הוא מיסר
אותו ולא באכזריות. כדכתיב וידעה עם לבבך. כי כאשר ייסר
איש את בנו ה" אלהיך מיסרך והיינו כרחמנות: על כן אל
יבעיט בהם. רק יצדיק דינו. כי צדיק וישר הוא. והב חסד
ואמת, שמיסר אותו בתחלה באמת ומרפא אותו בחסד, על כן

The royal preacher says: "All go unto one place;
all are of the dust, and all turn unto dust again. As
one dieth, so dieth the other." And serious indeed
is the alarming position of the hostage to death.
"Behold, happy is the man whom God correcteth, if
he despiseth not the chastisement of the Almighty;
for He maketh sore and bindeth up; He woundeth,
and His hands heal." For the chastisement inflicted
upon man frequently tends to his happiness and is
dispensed by Divine Providence commensurate with
man's strength to bear it, as it is written: "thou
shalt also consider in thy heart that as a man chast-
eneth his son, so the Almighty, thy God, chast-
eneth thee." We ought, therefore, not to burst forth
in murmurs and complaints at the Divine decrees,
but piously resign ourselves to the dispensation of
justice, and rather acknowledge that He is righteous
and just, and full of mercy and truth; that His visitations are in truth and His remedy is in mercy. We
must, therefore, humbly and filially submit to the

צריך לקבל עליו דין שמים באהבה, כי עיקר טובת האדם הוא
לעולם הבא:

ואמר רבא מי שיקבל עליו היסורין באהבה יראה זרע ויאריך
ימים, ותלמודו מתקיים בידו, שנאמר וחפץ ה" בידו יצליח: ואמר
רבא אמר רב הונא: אם רואה אדם שיסורין באין עליו, יפשפש
במעשיו שנאמר: נחפשה נחפשה דרכינו ונחקורה ונשובה אל ה":
פשפש ולא מצא, יתלה בבטול תורה, או ביסורין של אהבה.

---

punishment which the heavenly Judge deems proper
to entail upon us, since true happiness is only re-
served for a future world.

Ravah observes: "whoever submits to Divine
punishment with pious resignation, will behold his
offspring enjoy long life, and his previous study of
the Divine Law will be established; for Scripture
says: "with whom the Eternal is pleased, He bends
down by visiting him with sickness; he shall live
long, and through him that Law, which is the delight
of the Eternal, shall be firmly established and prosper." For the dispensation of Divine mercy, though
not understood by men, is nevertheless as just and
as upright as the Dispenser Himself.

The Rabbi continues in the name of Rabbi Hunah:
if a man perceives that affliction overtakes him, he
must search his past conduct; as it is written: "let
us search and try our ways, and return unto the
Eternal." If after searching he found nothing by
which he incurred punishment, he must attribute
it to the neglect of the study of the Word of God; or
look upon those visitations as springing from the love
of God, to try him and render him worthy of future

שנאמר: את אשר יאהב ה" יוכיח: שהקב'ה מדקדק עם הצדיקים
כחוט השערה, ליסר אותם עליהם כדי שיבא, זך ונקי לעולם הבא:
ואמר רבא אמר רב הונא, כל שהקב"ה חפץ בו מדכאו כיסורין
שנאמר וה" חפץ דכאו החלי: יכול אפילו לא קבלן מאהבה:
תלמוד לומר: אם תשים אשם נפשו: מה אשם לדעת אף יסורין
לדעת: כי יסורין שבאו לאדם בעבור חטאיו באים לו בעל כרחו.

---

bliss; for Scripture says: "for whom the Eternal
loveth, he correcteth." The Holy One (blessed be
He) visits at times with the greatest rigour the most
immaterial trespasses of His pious men, in order to
cleanse their souls from all iniquity, so that they
may enter in perfect purity the gates of everlasting
felicity. The same Rabbi continues to teach in the
name of Rabbi Hunah: he in whom the Almighty
delights is led to contrition of heart by severe affliction, as it is written: "in whom the Almighty delights
He bends down by visiting Him with sickness."
But these afflictions must be borne with resignation,
and the pious sufferer should, as in the words of our
text, deliver up his soul like a trespass-offering,
namely, as a trespass-offering is only efficacious
when brought with sincere repentance, so as to effect
reconciliation between man and his Maker, thus must
our sufferings be borne with pious submission, in
order to effect thereby forgiveness from God. Different, however, are the chastisements we receive as
punishment for sins committed, from those with which
heavenly love visits us as a trial to prove our fortitude. To the former we must implicitly submit,

אבל היסורין של אהבה, אם אינו מרוצה בהם יכול לסלקם
ממנו: כי הא דרבי יוחנן חלש, עאל לגביה רבי חנינא אמר
ליה: חביבין עליך יסורין, אמר לא הן ולא שכרן: אמר ליה:
הב לי ידך: יהב ליה ידיה, ואוקמיה: וכן רבי חייא אמר לא
הן ולא שכרן ואוקמיה: ורבי אלעזר חלש, אעל לגביה רבי
יוחנן, הוי דהוה קא גני בבית אפל, גלייה לדרעיה ונפל נהורא

whilst from the latter, we may hope to be relieved
by pious prayer offered to heaven on our behalf.
The Talmud Berachoth relates: Rabbi Haninah,
having visited Rabbi Jochanan in his illness, asked
his suffering friend: dost thou finally resign thyself
to these paternal chastisements? The sufferer rejoined: no, I would rather be without them and
without their eventual reward. In the course of
conversation he said: give me thy hand (inspire me
by thy instruction with fortitude and resignation);
Rabbi Haninah complied with this request, and
awakened within him a spirit of filial resignation and
firm submission to the unfathomable will of God.
The same success attended Rabbi Haninah on visiting Heeyah, who had also previously misunderstood
the Divine purpose in punishing him with heavy
afflictions. The Talmud relates another case, to
show that the lesson which Rabbi Jochanan derived
from the instruction of Rabbi Haninah was by him
most salutary applied to his colleague, Rabbi Elazar.
Rabbi Jochanan, on visiting Rabbi Elazar, saw that
he was stretched on his bed, which stood in a dark
chamber; Rabbi Jochanan uncovered his arm,* and

---

* The spirit of this allegory is, Rabbi Elazar was deficient of fortitude to
bear his sufferings. The words, "He slept in a dark chamber," indicate that

חייה דהוה קא בכי, אמר אמאי קא בכיה: אי משום תורה
דלא אפשת שנינו אהד המרבה ואחד הממעיט, ובלבד שיכין
לבו לשמים: ואי משום מזוני, לא כל האדם זוכה לשתי שולחנות:
אי משום בני, דין נרמא דעשיראי ביר: אמר להאי שופרא
דבלע בעפרא קא בכינא, אמר ליה על דא ודאי קא בכיה ובכי
תרייהו: אדהכי והכי אמר ליה, חביבין עליך יסורין: אמר ליה

suddenly tho chamber was illumined. He perceived
that Rabbi Elazar was weeping. Why weepest
thou? asked he. Is it because thou art prevented
by thy sufferings from promulgating the Law of God?
Our sages have already laid down the well grounded
maxim, that in our actions the quantity is immaterial,
if the quality is good, so that our heart is directed
to Him who is enthroneth in heaven. Or is it caused
by the anxiety for thy daily necessities? It is not
the lot of every man to feast at two tables (viz., the
enjoyment of terrestrial and celestial happiness). Is
it because thou art childless? Behold there the bone
of the tenth son whom I buried. No, said Rabbi
Elazar, I weep because of this bodily frame, the
beautiful work of an all-wise Creator, which must
now decompose into dust. Then answered Rabbi
Jochanan: thou hast cause to weep—both wept together. In the course of conversation Rabbi Jochanan asked him: dost thou finally resign thyself to
these paternal chastisements? The sufferer rejoined:

his mind was clouded in obscurity regarding the dispensation of punishment,
which he deemed undeserved. The teachings of Rabbi Jochanan, however,
who from experience learned how to submit to the Divine will, dispelled those
doubts, and enligtened the learned patient upon this subject. The uncovering
of his arm is a symbolical term for imparting instruction so clearly, that it
spread rays of light, comfort, composure and consolation.

לא הן ולא שכרן: אמר ליה הב לי ידך, הב לי ידיה ואוקמיה:
יכן רבי אלעזר קבל עליו יסורין על כפק הטא, באורתא אמר
בוא׳ אחי ורעי: ובצפרא אמר זילו, מפני בטול הורה: וכן רבי
קבל עליו יסורין:

———

7. אמרו חכמים: חייב אדם לברך על הרעה כשם שמברך
על הטובה׃ שנאמר: ואהבת את ה״ אלהיך בכל לבבך׃ בשני
יצריך ׃ ביצר טוב וביצר הרע׃ ובכל נפשך ׃ אפילו הוא נוטל את

———

no, I would rather dispense with them and with
their eventual reward. After a pause he said: support me with thy hand (viz., inspire me by thy instruction with fortitude and resignation). He complied with his request, and successfully. Rabbi
Elazar likewise submitted willingly to the Divine
punishment, which he thought he might have incurred
by some sin unknown to him. At evening he hailed
his sufferings with the exclamation: welcome ye, my
brethren and friends! but at dawn they were soothed
by the meditation of the Law; viz., his mind was so
absorbed in the word of God, that he became un-
conscious of his bodily sufferings.

———

The sages observe: man is in duty bound to bless
God for evil as well as for the good he receives from
Providence; for it is said: "and thou shalt love the
Eternal thy God with all thy heart, with all thy soul
and with all thy might." With all thy heart, signifies with both thy inclinations, viz., that which is
prone to evil, and that which adheres to do good;
with all thy soul, implies: thou art bound to thank

נפשך · ובכל מאודך · בכל ממונך: ד"א בכל מדה ומדה שהוא
מודד לך. הוה מודה לו במאוד מאוד: מאי מברך. על הטובה
אומר: ברוך הטוב והמטיב: ועל שמועות רעות אומר: ברוך דיין
האמת: וחייב לקבלינהו בשמחה: מנא הני מילי אמר רבה בר בר
חנה אמר רבי יוחנן. דאמר קרא בה" אהלל דבר. באלהים אהלל
דבר. רבי אבוהו אמר מהכא. חסד ומשפט אשירה לך ה" אזמרה:
רבי תנחום אומר · צרה ויגון אמצא · ושם ה" אקרא · רבנן אמרי ·
אמר קרא: ה" נתן וה" לקח יהי שם ה" מבורך: אמר רב הונא

God, should it even please Divine Providence to deprive thee of life; and with all thy might signifies
with all temporal substance. According to some, the
words "and with all thy might" signify, with whatever
measure He metes out His dispensation unto thee, do
thou thank Him as much as thy might possibly per-
mits thee. With the only difference that, at a good
occurrence, man must say: blessed be He who deals
with us so exceedingly kind; but, at an unfortunate
event, he must say: blessed be the true Judge, and
bear the affliction with joyful and pious resignation.
Rabbi Bar Bar-Chanah deduces the above-mentioned
doctrine in the name of Rabbi Jochanan, from the
scriptural passage which says: "in God will I praise
His words, in the Eternal will I praise His words."
Rabbi Abbuha infers it from the following passage:
"I will praise Thee both for mercy and judgment;
unto Thee, O Eternal, will I sing." Rabbi Tanhum
proves it from the following verse: "I found trouble
and sorrow; then called I upon the name of the
Eternal." But the sages say: Scripture tells us
very distinctly: "the Eternal gave and the Eternal
hath taken away, blessed be the name of the

אמר רב: וכן תנא משמיה דרבי עקיבא: לעולם יהא אדם רגיל
לומר: כל מה דעביד רחמנא. לטב עביד: ויקבל עליו כל מה
שאירע לו באהבה. וכמו שאמר איוב: גם את הטוב נקבל מאת
האלהים ואת הרע לא נקבל: כי מי יודע מי שהוא לטובת
האדם או לרעה לו: לפעמים יחשוב האדם שהוא לטובת
הטובה שבא לו. ולבסוף נמצא שהוא לרעתו. וכן להיפך.
שיגיע לאדם צרה אף שהיא גדולה מאוד: ואף על פי כן יכול
להיות. שהקב"ה עשה לו כל זה לטובתו. ואף אם ימות.
כדכתיב מפני הרעה נאסף הצדיק. וכמו שמצינו ביאשיה המלך.

Eternal." Rabbi Hunah teaches in the name of
Raave (some teach in the name of Rabbi Akiba):
man should at all times accustom himself to say:
everything which the heavenly and merciful Providence ordains for man tends merely to his felicity, and
every affliction, however severe, should be borne
with fortitude, patience and pious resignation, agreeably to the words of the pious sufferer Job, who
said: "what, shall we receive good at the hand of
God, and shall we not receive evil?" For where is
the mortal that can with certainty say: this tends to
man's good and that to his evil? Do we not look
upon many incidents as upon a real happiness, yet
how grievously disappointed are we afterwards to
behold this apparent success turned into an actual
disaster? And again, do we not oftentimes deem
ourselves plunged into the deepest misery, whilst
the Holy One (blessed be He) destines it for our
good? In such a view, son of man, thou art to look
upon the pangs of death, as Scripture says: "previous to the evil, the righteous is taken away." The

אַף שֶׁנֶּהֱרַג וְעָשׂוּ כָל גּוּפוֹ כִּכְבָרָה. טוֹבָה הָיָה לוֹ שֶׁלֹּא רָאָה
בְּחֻרְבַּן הַבַּיִת:

וְהִנֵּה מִי גֶבֶר יִחְיֶה וְלֹא יִרְאֶה מָוֶת: כְּמוֹ שֶׁאָמְרוּ הַחֲכָמִים:
הַיְלוֹדִים לָמוּת וְהַמֵּתִים לְהַחֲיוֹת: כִּי כָל אָדָם יוֹדֵעַ מִיָּד כְּשֶׁנּוֹלָד.
שֶׁסּוֹפוֹ לָמוּת. וְעַל כָּרְחוֹ הוּא נוֹלָד. כִּי הַנְּשָׁמָה הִיא לְמַעְלָה
בְּטוֹבָה. שֶׁנֶּהֱנֵית מִזִּיו הַשְּׁכִינָה עַל כֵּן אֵינָה רוֹצָה לֵירֵד לְמַטָּה

---

pious king Josiah died a most awful death, in order
that he might not behold the overthrow of his kingdom and the destruction of the temple, which
assuredly would have been more painful to him than
the severe strokes of death which were inflicted on
him; for tradition tells us that the arrows of the
archers perforated his body, and made it like a sieve.

Behold, says king David; what man is there that
liveth and shall not see death? Agreeably to this
maxim, our sages of yore remark: those who are
born must die, and those who are dead will be re-
vived. Yea, every man is conscious of this awful
truth, viz., that from the cradle we unceasingly
verge towards the grave, whether willingly or not;
for as man is born without his consent, he is doomed
to die, however violently he may struggle against it.
The soul of man, ere she was sent down to inhabit
the tabernacle of clay, and before she was wrapt up
in earthly coils, enjoys bliss most exquisite in the
spiritual regions. There she feasts on the glory of
the Divine presence, and from thence this heavenly
daughter but reluctantly descends to be imprisoned
in the body of frail mortal. But the Holy One

בגוף האדם: והקב"ה נותנה בגוף האדם כדי לקבל יותר שלימות
וטובת עולם הבא. אם יזכה כי נתן הקב"ה הבחירה לאדם. כי
בטרם נתנה בגוף. הנשמות כולם במזג השוה בטובה מצד החסד
אבל אהר ביאתה בגוף יכולה לקנית יותר טובת עולם הבא מצד
האמה שעושה בעולם הזה לקיים מצות בוראה ותורתו. מה שאין
כן לעשות לה מקודם זה בעולם הנשמות. ועל כן כשנשמה
הצדיק נפרדה מהגוף או היא מאירה יותר בעולם העליון ומהעננת

(blessed be He) deemed proper to join the immortal
soul with a mortal frame, in order that man may, by
virtue of his own merit and activity, render himself
more deserving and more worthy of everlasting happiness. The attainment of this perfection depends,
however, entirely upon himself, since he is, by the
infinite mercy of God, endowed with the power of
free agency. All souls, before they are breathed
into the nostrils of earthly beings, are of equal origin
and, by the mercy of God, enjoy equally celestial
bliss. But after their being sent down to the terrestrial world to inhabit the body of frail man, they
can render themselves worthy of higher bliss by
virtue of truth, for the practice of which they have
ample scope in this world; and by obeying and ful-
filling the behests and laws of the Creator, they
acquire a perfection which it is impossible to reach
in the region of spirits, since this high rank can only
be attained by unremitting labor, which is not the
lot of the celestial inhabitants. Hence it is that the
soul of the truly pious, after being separated from
her earthly frame, becometh more perfect, more
pure, more radiant than before. There she shineth

בעדן העליון מאשר היה לה מקדמה דנא: וכשם שאין בנשמות
להוסיף בשלמות קודם שבאו לעולם הזה. כך אין בהם כח
לקנות שלמות אחר שנפטרים מעולם הזה לעולם הבא וכן אמר
רבי יעקב. העולם הזה דומה לפרוזדור בפני העולם הבא התקן
עצמך בפרוזדור כדי שתכנס לטרקלין: הוא היה אומר יפה שעה
אחת של קורת רוח בעולם הבא מכל חיי עולם הזה. ויפה
שעה אחת בתשובה ובמעשים טובים בעולם הזה מכל חיי עולם

more gloriously in the celestial spheres; there she
enjoys higher felicity in the garden of Eden, in the
abode of true gladness and everlasting felicity. But
as well as the soul, before she has been sent down
to occupy the house of clay, cannot render herself
more perfect, or to elevate herself to a higher degree,
or to add aught to her primitive dignity, in a like
manner is the soul unable to attain a higher perfection, or to render herself worthy of a sublimer
state, after having quitted this world for that to
come. This idea is very laconically and aptly expressed by Rabbi Jacob. This world, says the
Rabbi, may be compared to a vestibule before the
future world; prepare thyself, therefore, in the
vestibule, that thou mayest enter the palace. He
used to say: *one* hour employed in repentance and
good deeds in this world is far preferable to a whole
life in the future one; and *one* hour's mental delight
in the future world is preferable to a whole life in
this world.

הבא: על כן אין לאדם בעולם הזה אלא לסגל מצות ומעשים
טובים כדי ׳שיזכה לשכר הטוב המתוקן לעד לעולם הבא. וכל
מה שיבא עליו מן השמים יקבל באהבה בהשגחת ה״ עליו ליסרו
לטובתו ויצדיק דינו. ואו אף שנגזר עליו לרעה יהפכנו ה״ לטובה
דכתיב הפכת מספדי למחול לי פתחת שקי ותאזרני שמחה:

Man should, therefore, as long as he abides on
earth, endeavor to fulfil the commandments of the
Eternal, and practise virtue and piety, in order to
render himself deserving of the great reward stored
up for the righteous in the future world. Bear
therefore thou, my devout brother and sister, every
vicissitude sent by heaven, with pious resignation,
fortitude and filial submission! Look upon them as
visitations sent by an all-wise and divine Providence,
which destines thine improvement. Acknowledge
that the heavenly Father is the most high and true
Judge, and He will surely change all evil decrees
pending over thee into grace and mercy, and thou
wilt ultimately exclaim joyously in the words of the
royal bard: "Thou hast turned my wailing tones
from me into dancing glees; thou hast put off my
sackcloth, and girdled me with gladness."

After the "learning" of the Talmudical portion, the following
prayer is to be pronounced:

אָנָּא יְיָ מֶלֶךְ מָלֵא רַחֲמִים, אֲשֶׁר בְּיָדְךָ נֶפֶשׁ

כָּל־חָי וְרוּחַ כָּל־בְּשַׂר אִישׁ, יְהִי־נָא לְרָצוֹן לְפָנֶיךָ

תַּלְמוּד תּוֹרָתֵנוּ וּתְפִלָּתֵנוּ בַּעֲבוּר נִשְׁמַת (פלוני בר

או בת פלונית,) וּגְמָל־נָא עָלֶיהָ בְּחַסְדְּךָ הַגָּדוֹל לִפְתּוֹחַ

לָהּ שַׁעֲרֵי רַחֲמִים וָחֶסֶד וְשַׁעֲרֵי גַן עֵדֶן, וּתְקַבֵּל

אוֹתָהּ בְּאַהֲבָה וְחִבָּה, וּשְׁלַח לָהּ מַלְאָכֶיךָ הַקְּדוֹשִׁים

לְהוֹלִיכָהּ וּלְהוֹשִׁיבָהּ תַּחַת עֵץ הַחַיִּים אֵצֶל נִשְׁמוֹת

הַצַּדִּיקִים וְהַצַּדְקָנִיּוֹת הַחֲסִידִים וְהַחֲסִידוֹת,

לֵהָנוֹת מִזִּיו שְׁכִינָתֶךָ, לְהִתְעַנֵּג מִטּוּבְךָ הַצָּפוּן

לַצַּדִּיקִים, וּלְהַשְׂבִּיעָהּ שֹׂבַע שְׂמָחוֹת אֶת־פָּנֶיךָ:

וְהַגּוּף יָנוּחַ בַּקֶּבֶר בִּמְנוּחָה נְכוֹנָה בְּהַשְׁקֵט וּבְבִטְחָה

וּבְשָׁלוֹם, וְיִישַׁן שְׁנָתוֹ כְּנַחַת, וְלֹא יֵעָצֵב וְלֹא יִבָּהֵל

וְלֹא יִרְגַּז מִמִּשְׁכָּבוֹ, כְּמוֹ שֶׁכָּתוּב, יָבוֹא שָׁלוֹם

יָנוּחוּ עַל־מִשְׁכְּבוֹתָם הֹלֵךְ נְכֹחוֹ, וְכָתוּב יַעַלְזוּ

חֲסִידִים בְּכָבוֹד יְרַנְּנוּ עַל־מִשְׁכְּבוֹתָם, וְכָתוּב אִם־

תִּשְׁכַּב לֹא תִפְחָד וְשָׁכַבְתָּ וְעָרְבָה שְׁנָתֶךָ:

After the "learning" of the Talmudical portion, the following
prayer is to be pronounced:

We beseech Thee, O Eternal, most merciful King, in whose hand is the soul of every living being, and the breath of all flesh; may our meditation on Thy sacred law and prayer on behalf of the soul of the departed (*here the name of the deceased is mentioned*) be acceptable in Thy presence. Requite unto her according to the bounty of Thine infinite kindness. O open unto her the gates of mercy and compassion which lead to the garden of Eden, and receive her in loving kindness. Send unto her Thy holy ministering angels to bear her to, and to seat her beneath the tree of life; there to join the souls of the righteous, virtuous and pious; there to feast in the brightness of Thy glory, and satisfy her with Thy bounty, treasured up for the just. O may even the body of the departed repose in peace, in gladness, in joy, as vouchsafed by Thy holy prophet: "He shall enter into peace. They shall rest on their couches, each one who walketh uprightly." And as it is predicted by the inspired Psalmist: "Let the pious be joyful in Glory; let them sing aloud upon their couches." And as it is promised by the wisest of kings: "when thou liest down thou shalt not fear, and thy sleep shall be sweet."

לזכר.

אָנָּא תִּסְלַח וְתִמְחַל
לוֹ עַל־כָּל־פְּשָׁעָיו, כִּי
אָדָם אֵין צַדִּיק בָּאָרֶץ
אֲשֶׁר יַעֲשֶׂה־טּוֹב וְלֹא
יֶחֱטָא, וּזְכָר־לוֹ זְכִיּוֹתָיו
וְצִדְקוֹתָיו אֲשֶׁר עָשָׂה,
וְהַשְׁפִּיעַ לוֹ מִנִּשְׁמָתוֹ
לְדַשֵּׁן עַצְמוֹתָיו בַּקֶּבֶר
מֵרַב טוּב הַצָּפוּן לַצַּדִּיקִים
כְּמוֹ שֶׁכָּתוּב, מָה רַב
טוּבְךָ אֲשֶׁר־צָפַנְתָּ
לִירֵאֶיךָ, זְכָתוּב שֹׁמֵר
כָּל־עַצְמֹתָיו אַחַת מֵהֵנָּה
לֹא נִשְׁבָּרָה, וְיִשְׁכֹּן בֶּטַח
בָּדָד וְשַׁאֲנַן מִפַּחַד רָעָה
וְלֹא יִרְאֶה פְּנֵי גֵי־דִהנֹּם.
וְנִשְׁמָתוֹ תְּהִי צְרוּרָה
בִּצְרוֹר הַחַיִּים וּלְהַחֲיוֹתוֹ

לנקבה.

אָנָּא תִּסְלַח וְתִמְחַל
לָהּ עַל־כָּל־פְּשָׁעֶיהָ, כִּי
אָדָם אֵין צַדִּיק בָּאָרֶץ
אֲשֶׁר יַעֲשֶׂה־טּוֹב וְלֹא
יֶחֱטָא, וּזְכָר־לָהּ זְכִיּוֹתֶיהָ
וְצִדְקוֹתֶיהָ אֲשֶׁר עָשְׂתָה,
וְתַשְׁפִּיעַ לָהּ מִנִּשְׁמָתָהּ
לְדַשֵּׁן עַצְמוֹתֶיהָ בַּקֶּבֶר
מֵרַבטוּב הַצָּפוּן לַצַּדִּיקִים,
כְּמוֹ שֶׁכָּתוּב, מָה רַב
טוּבְךָ אֲשֶׁר־צָפַנְתָּ
לִירֵאֶיךָ, וְכָתוּב שֹׁמֵר
כָּל־עַצְמֹתָיו אַחַת מֵהֵנָּה
לֹא נִשְׁבָּרָה, וְתִשְׁכֹּן בֶּטַח
בָּדָד וְשַׁאֲנָן מִפַּחַד רָעָה,
וְלֹא תִרְאֶה פְּנֵי גֵי־דִהנָּם,
וְנִשְׁמָתָהּ תְּהִי צְרוּרָה
בִּצְרוֹר הַחַיִּים וּלְהַחֲיוֹתָהּ

Thou, merciful God, pardon and forgive [him] [her] all [his] [her] iniquities, for surely there is not a just person upon earth, who doeth good and sinneth not; but remember unto [him] [her] the meritorious and benevolent deeds of [his] [her] life.

O gracious Father, grant in Thine infinite mercy that the mortal frame and decayed bones, whilst in the grave, may partake of Thine endless bounty, vouchsafed unto [his] [her] immortal soul, of the goodness treasured up for the righteous, in accordance with the divine psalmist: "O how great Thy goodness which Thou hast laid up for those who fear Thee. And again it is said: "He who keepeth all his bones, not one of them is broken." O grant that the departed may dwell safely, in quietude, free from the terror of evil, from the presence of גיהנם. May [his] [her] soul be bound up in the bundle of life everlasting, and quicken [him] [her] at the time

בִּתְחִיַת הַמֵּתִים עִם כָּל־ בִּתְחִיַת הַמֵּתִים עִם כָּל־
מֵתֵי עַמְּךָ יִשְׂרָאֵל. אָמֵן: מֵתֵי עַמְּךָ יִשְׂרָאֵל. אָמֵן:

After the recital of the prayer, the following Kaddish,
(קדיש דרבנן) is said:

יִתְגַּדַּל וְיִתְקַדַּשׁ שְׁמֵהּ רַבָּא בְּעָלְמָא דִּי־בְרָא
כִרְעוּתֵהּ וְיַמְלִיךְ מַלְכוּתֵהּ בְּחַיֵּיכוֹן וּבְיוֹמֵיכוֹן וּבְחַיֵּי
דְכָל בֵּית יִשְׂרָאֵל בַּעֲגָלָא וּבִזְמַן קָרִיב וְאִמְרוּ אָמֵן:
יְהֵא שְׁמֵהּ רַבָּא מְבָרַךְ לְעָלַם וּלְעָלְמֵי עָלְמַיָּא ·
יִתְבָּרַךְ וְיִשְׁתַּבַּח וְיִתְפָּאַר וְיִתְרוֹמַם וְיִתְנַשֵּׂא וְיִתְהַדָּר
וְיִתְעַלֶּה וְיִתְהַלָּל שְׁמֵהּ דְּקוּדְשָׁא בְּרִיךְ הוּא לְעֵלָּא
מִן־כָּל־בִּרְכָתָא וְשִׁירָתָא תֻּשְׁבְּחָתָא וְנֶחָמָתָא
דַּאֲמִירָן בְּעָלְמָא וְאִמְרוּ אָמֵן:

עַל־יִשְׂרָאֵל וְעַל־רַבָּנָן, וְעַל־תַּלְמִידֵיהוֹן וְעַל־כָּל־
תַּלְמִידֵי תַלְמִידֵיהוֹן, וְעַל־כָּל־מַן דְּעָסְקִין בְּאוֹרַיְתָא,
דִּי בְּאַתְרָא הָדֵן וְדִי בְּכָל־אֲתַר וַאֲתַר, יְהֵא לְהוֹן
וּלְכוֹן שְׁלָמָא רַבָּא חִנָּא וְחִסְדָּא וְרַחֲמִין וְחַיִּין
אֲרִיכִין וּמְזוֹנָא רְוִיחָא וּפוּרְקָנָא מִן־קֳדָם אֲבוּהוֹן
דְּשְׁמַיָּא וְאַרְעָא וְאִמְרוּ אָמֵן:

of the resurrection of the dead, with all the departed
of Thy people Israel.   Amen.

After the recital of the prayer, the following Kaddish,
(קריש דרבנן), is said:

May the great name of the Eternal be exalted and
sanctified throughout all the world which He created
according to His will; and may He establish His
kingdom in your life-time and in your days, and in
the life-time of the whole house of Israel, speedily
and without delay, and say ye: Amen.

(*Cong.*)   Amen.   May His omnipotent name be
blessed, for ever and over, throughout the world.

(*Reader.*)   May His hallowed name be praised,
glorified, extolled, magnified and honored, and most
excellently adored in expressions far surpassing all
blessings, hymns, praises and comforts, that can be
expressed in the world, and say ye: Amen.

Unto Israel, their masters, their disciples and all
their successors, who assiduously study the holy
law, who are in this and every other place; may
there be fulness of peace, favor and mercy, compassion, long and happy life, ample sustenance, and
redemption from all evil, from the presence of the
Sovereign of heaven and earth, both to them and
you, and say ye: Amen.

יְהֵא שְׁלָמָא רַבָּא מִן־שְׁמַיָּא וְחַיִּים (טוֹבִים) עָלֵינוּ
וְעַל־כָּל־יִשְׂרָאֵל וְאִמְרוּ אָמֵן:

וִיהִי שֵׁם יְיָ מְבוֹרָךְ מֵעַתָּה וְעַד עוֹלָם:

עֹשֶׂה שָׁלוֹם בִּמְרוֹמָיו הוּא יַעֲשֶׂה שָׁלוֹם עָלֵינוּ וְעַל־
כָּל־יִשְׂרָאֵל וְאִמְרוּ אָמֵן:

עֶזְרִי מֵעִם יְיָ עֹשֵׂה שָׁמַיִם וָאָרֶץ:

תחנות על הקברים.

AT THE GRAVES OF VARIOUS RELATIVES.

אָמַרְתְּ לַיהֹוָה אֲדֹנָי אָתָּה טוֹבָתִי בַּל־עָלֶיךָ:
לִקְדוֹשִׁים אֲשֶׁר־בָּאָרֶץ הֵמָּה וְאַדִּירֵי כָּל־חֶפְצִי־
בָם:

על קבר של נקבה.	על קבר של זכר.
הִנְנִי בָאתִי עַל־קִבְרֵךְ	הִנְנִי בָאתִי עַל־קִבְרְךָ
לִכְבוֹד הַקָּדוֹשׁ בָּרוּךְ	לִכְבוֹד הַקָּדוֹשׁ בָּרוּךְ הוּא
הוּא וְלִכְבוֹדֵךְ וְלִכְבוֹד נִשְׁמָתֵךְ	וְלִכְבוֹדְךָ וְלִכְבוֹד נִשְׁמָתֶךָ
נִשְׁמָתֵךְ, כִּי אַהֲבַת עוֹלָם	כִּי אַהֲבַת עוֹלָם אֲהַבְתִּיךָ
אֲהַבְתִּיךְ: עַל־כֵּן בָּאתִי	עַל־כֵּן בָּאתִי עַתָּה
עַתָּה לִמְקוֹם שְׁכִינָתֵךְ.	לִמְקוֹם שְׁכוּנָתֶךָ.

(*Reader.*) May abundance of peace and happy life be bestowed upon us and upon all Israel, and say ye: Amen.

(*Cong.*) Blessed be the name of the Eternal from henceforth and for evermore.

(*Reader.*) May He who establisheth peace in His high heavens, grant, through His mercy, peace to us and all Israel, and say ye: Amen.

(*Cong.*) My relief is from the Eternal, who made the heaven and earth.

PRAYERS AT THE GRAVES.

AT THE GRAVES OF VARIOUS RELATIVES.

Arise, O my soul! elevate thyself to thy God in heaven. Say thou unto the Eternal: Thou art my Lord; naught excelleth Thee. As to the holy that are in the land, and the mighty nobles in them, are all my delights.

Glory to the most Holy One (blessed be He). Peace to thine ashes, and glory to thy soul. [*Here mention the name and relationship of the deceased, as, for instance: brother, sister, uncle, or aunt.*] I ap-

לְהִתְפַּלֵּל עַל־קִבְרְךָ, לְהִתְפַּלֵל עַל־קִבְרֶךָ, אֶל־
אֶל־־יוֹצֵר נִשְׁמָתֶךָ. יוֹצֵר נִשְׁמָתֶךָ. שֶׁתִּתְעַדֵּן
שֶׁתִּתְעַדֵּן בְּעֵדֶן אֱלֹהֶיךָ. בְּעֵדֶן אֱלֹהֶיךָ. עִם־נִשְׁמוֹת
עִם נִשְׁמוֹת אֲבוֹתֶיךָ. אֲבוֹתֶיךָ בְּחֶמְלַת יְיָ
בְּחֶמְלַת יְיָ אֱלֹהֶיךָ.לְהַשְׂבִּיעַ אֱלֹהֶיךָ. לְהַשְׂבִּיעַ מִטּוּבוֹ
מִטּוּבוֹ לְנִשְׁמָתֶךָ. לְנִשְׁמָתֶךָ.בְּשֶׂבַע שְׂמָחוֹת
בְּשֶׂבַע שְׂמָחֹת לְשִׂמְחָתֶךָ. לְשִׂמְחָתֶךָ. וּלְהַחֲלִיץ
וּלְהַחֲלִיץ בְּקִבְרֶךָ בְּקִבְרֶךָ עַצְמוֹתֶיךָ. וּמֵרַב
עַצְמוֹתֶיךָ. וּמֵרַב טוּב הַצָּפוּן לַצַּדִּיקִים
הַצָּפוּן לַצַּדִּיקִים לְהַשְׁפִּיעֶךָ. וּמִטַּלּוּ
לְהַשְׁפִּיעֶךָ. וּמִטַּלּוּ לְהוֹרִיד עַל־רֹאשֶׁךָ.
לְהוֹרִיד עַל־רֹאשֶׁךָ. וּבִתְחִיַּת הַמֵּתִים
וּבִתְחִיַּת הַמֵּתִים לְהַחֲיוֹתֶךָ: וְגַם אַתְּ
לְהַחֲיוֹתֶךָ. וְגַם אַתָּה תִּגְמְלִי עָלַי חַסְדֵּךְ.
תִּגְמֹל עָלַי חַסְדֶּךָ. כַּאֲשֶׁר הָיִית אֲהוּבָתִי
כַּאֲשֶׁר הָיִיתָ אֲהוּבִי בְּחַיֶּיךָ. לְהִתְפַּלֵּל בַּעֲדִי
בְּחַיֶּיךָ. לְהִתְפַּלֵּל בַּעֲדִי וּלְהִתְחַנֵּן לְיוֹצְרֵךְ.
וּלְהִתְחַנֵּן לְיוֹצְרֶךָ.לְהֵטִיב לְהֵטִיב עִמִּי בִּזְכוּתֵךְ.
עִמִּי בִּזְכוּתֶךָ. וּבִזְכוּת וּבִזְכוּת כָּל־הַשּׁוֹכְבִים

proach tremblingly thy grave, for I love thee with an everlasting love. Hither have I repaired, to pour out my heart in prayer before the God of all spirits, to bestow on thy soul His infinite and tender mercies, to delight thee in the garden of Eden, and to gladden thee with His pure and celestial joy amongst thy departed and beatified forefathers.

O may the God of glory, in His unbounded compassion, take thee under His divine protection, and grant thee fulness of joy and unclouded glory, from the abundance of good which He hath in secret laid up for the righteous and virtuous, and to refresh and strengthen thy weary and languishing bones in the graves, as the heavenly dew revives the drooping and withered plants.

I feel that the sympathy which thou hast felt, and the attachment thou hast cherished for me, whilst alive on earth, have neither become chilled by separation nor extinct by death; and as I now pour out my heart and soul for thee to the merciful Father in

כָּל־הַשּׁוֹכְבִים בִּשְׁכוּנָתֶךָ. בִּשְׁכוּנָתֶךָ. לְקַבֵּל
לְקַבֵּל תְּפִלָּתִי עִם־ תְּבִלָּתִי עִם־תְּפִלָּתֶךָ.
תְּפִלָּתֶךָ. לְהָפֵר כָּל־ לְהָפֵר כָּל־גְּזֵרוֹת רָעוֹת
גְּזֵרוֹת רָעוֹת מִמֶּנִּי וּמִכָּל־ מִמֶּנִּי וּמִכָּל־קְרוֹבֶיךָ:
קְרוֹבֶיךָ:

וְאַתָּה אֱלֹהֵי אֲשֶׁר נֶפֶשׁ הַחַיִּים וְהַמֵּתִים בְּיָדֶךָ.
תְּקַבֵּל תְּפִלָּתֵנוּ לְפָנֶי כִסֵּא כְבוֹדֶךָ. וְאַל־תְּשִׁיבֵנוּ
רֵיקָם מִלְפָנֶיךָ. שַׂמַּח תְּשַׂמַּח אֶת־נֶפֶשׁ עֲבָדֶיךָ.
וּבָרֵךְ עֲבָדֶיךָ מִבִּרְכוֹתֶיךָ. לִרְאוֹת בְּטוֹבַת עוֹלָמֶךָ:

ON THE ANNIVERSARY OF THE DEATH
OF PARENTS. *(Jahrzeit.)*

שָׁלוֹם עָלַיִךְ נִשְׁמָה טְהוֹרָה. כְּנֵר מֵאֲבוּקָה
הוּדְלָקָה לְהָאִירָה. אֵינֶנָּה מִן־הַיְסוֹדוֹת וְלֹא
כְהִשְׁתַּלְשְׁלוּת הַשְּׂכָלִים הַנִּפְרָדִים. רַק בְּרִיָּה
בִּפְנֵי עַצְמָהּ בְּרוּחָנִיּוּת וְלֹא בְּאֵבָרִים וְגִידִים. עֶצֶם
נִבְדָּל הִיא טָהוֹר וְקָדוֹשׁ מִקַּדְמֵי אֶרֶץ וְלֵאלֹהִים
מְשֻׁבַּחַת. וְסוֹגֶרֶת עוֹמֶרֶת קֹדֶם הֲיַת הָאָדָם כְּאֶחָד
מִצְבָא מָרוֹם וּמֵהֶם נִכְבָּדֶת. וּכְרֹב חַסְדֵּי הָאֵל
בְּרִאוֹתָהּ נֶהֱנֵית מִזִּיו הַשְּׁכִינָה בְּמַתְּנַת חִנָּם,

heaven, so let thy beatified immortal spirit appear before Him to implore mercy upon us on earth.

And Thou, O God, in whose hand are the souls of the living and the dead, may He deign to hear our united prayers, and remove from me and from all my relatives and friends every evil decree. May our prayers ascend Thy glorious throne, and dismiss us not fruitlessly from Thy presence. Surely Thou wilt rejoice the soul of Thy servant and bless him from Thy blessings, and grant that we may be worthy to behold Thine everlasting felicity. Amen.

ON THE ANNIVERSARY OF THE DEATH OF PARENTS. *(Jahrzeit.)*

Peace, peace to thee [beloved father] [affectionate mother]; peace be to thy pious soul, that heavenly spark from the eternal flame, that now rests with God. Peace to thy ashes that repose here. Verily, with thee reigns peace; with me, alas! is grief and sorrow. For since thou hast gone from me, true joy has almost forsaken me. Daily does my anguish grow stronger; with the increase of time I more keenly feel what I have lost in thee, thou purified soul, whose life, whose actions, whose longing, whose ardent affection have entirely and solely been devoted to my weal and happiness. But, alas! it has pleased God, in His inscrutable wisdom, to deprive me of the crown of my glory. My eye does no

וְשָׂכָר אֵין לָהּ חֵלֶף עֲבוֹדָתָהּ אַחֲרֵי שֶׁמְּכֻרְחַת
בִּפְעוּלָתָהּ כִּשְׁאָר כָּל־בְּרוּאֵי מַעֲלָה שֶׁבְּטִבְעָם הִיא
הַפְּעוּלָה בְּלִי רָצוֹן וּבְחִירָה . עַל־כֵּן נִתָּנָה לָאָרֶץ
בְּתוֹךְ חֹמֶר הַגּוּף, לִהְיוֹת בַּעֲלַת בְּחִירָה מָאוֹס
בָּרַע וּבָחוֹר בְּטוֹב. כְּדֵי לְזַכּוֹתָהּ יוֹתֵר מִן־הַמַּלְאָכִים,
לְהָרִים קַרְנָהּ וּלְשַׁלֵּם לָהּ טוֹב שֶׁעָסְקָה בֶּאֱמוּנָה .
וְגַם לֹא יֶחְסַר בְּרִיָּה יְשָׁרָה כָּזוֹ מִן הָעוֹלָם, כִּי הִיא
עוֹלָה עַל־כָּל־בְּרוּאֵי מַטָּה וּמַעֲלָה שֶׁהֵם פּוֹעֲלִים
בְּטִבְעָם וַדַרְכָּם . וְהָאָדָם הוּא בַּעַל בְּחִירָה בְּלִי
הֶכְרֵחַ בְּעֶרְכּוֹ וּמִפְּנֵי כְּבוֹד הַבּוֹרֵא מְעַנֶּה וּמְסַגֵּף
עַצְמוֹ בְּמוֹרָא . וּבוֹחֵר בְּצַעַר וְהֶפְסֵד גּוּפוֹ, לְקַבֵּל
שָׂכָר טוֹב כִּפְלַיִם וְלֵהָנוֹת מִזִּיו הַשְּׁכִינָה: וְאַתְּ
נִשְׁמָה טְהוֹרָא, כְּלִבְנַת הַסַּפִּיר מְאִירָה . בְּעֵדֶן
גַּן אֱלֹהִים אַתְּ, וְתֵשְׁבִי בְּמַעֲלוֹת הַקְּדוֹשִׁים וּטְהוֹרִים
צַדִּיקִים וַחֲסִידִים וִישָׁרִים. צְרוּרָה אַתְּ בִּצְרוֹר
הַחַיִּים כְּהֵיכַל יְיָ חַי וְקַיָּם. וַאֲנִי מִיּוֹם אֲשֶׁר עֲזַבְתִּנִי
לֹא נָחַתִּי וְלֹא שָׁלַוְתִּי וְלֹא שָׁקַטְתִּי מִלְּהִתְאַבֵּל בְּלִבִּי
עָלַיִךְ. כִּי יְכוֹלָה הָיִית לְזַכֵּנִי, וּמְטוּבֵךְ לְהֵטִיבֵנִי: אַךְ
רְצוֹן הָאֵל הוּא לְקַבֵּל תַּנְחוּמִים, שֶׁלֹּא יֹאמְרוּ הֲרַב כַּמָּה

more see thy venerable and dignified countenance;
my ear no more hears thy sweet, tender and affectionate instruction, and thy consoling words. Thou art
gone to eternity, and I, unhappy one, have [no father]
[no mother] on earth to guide my steps and to direct
my counsels. Alas! my heart breaks because of
grief, and my eyes suffuse and melt with tears because
of my sins. Never, never shall I see thee on earth!
Yet, be not cast down, thou my soul! I shall again
behold thee [beloved father] [affectionate mother]
in yonder celestial abode, where thou now art re-
posing, in the presence of thy heavenly Maker.
Blessed soul of my [father] [mother]! How great is
my delight in hoping to be eternally with thee, without fear of a sorrowful separation.

I do, therefore, on this solemn day of the anniversary of thy earthly departure, here, at the sacred
shrine that contains thy mortal remains, fully determine to regulate and improve my future days, so
that I may render myself worthy of enduring thy
glorious presence on that great and awful day of the
Eternal, when the hearts of children will be restored
to parents. I sincerely determine to walk in the
path of rectitude, piety and virtue. I will never
desecrate thy unsullied name, or profane thy dear
memory by an ungodly action.

קָשֶׁה וַיְכַל אֶת אֲשֶׁר עָשָׂה. עַל־כֵּן חַיָּב הָאָדָם.
לְהִתְנַחֵם וְלֵאמֹר גְּזַר יְיָ הוּא אֲשֶׁר גָּזַר עַל כָּל־
הָאָדָם. אָמְנָם בְּהַגִּיעַ תֹּר יוֹם זֵכֶר מִיתָתְךָ מִדֵּי
שָׁנָה בְשָׁנָה, אֶזְכְּרָה אֱלֹהִים וְאֶהֱמָיָה לֵאמֹר צֵא
וּרְאֵי, שֶׁמָּא מַזָּל־יוֹם אוֹ מַזָּל־שָׁעָה גָּרַם לַבֹּקֶר
הַפְּנֵקֶס לִפְנֵי חוֹקֵר וְסוֹקֵר הַכֹּל. וְיוֹם זֶה הַגַּלְגַּל
סָבֵב הַחוֹבָה, אֲשֶׁר אֵשׁ יָצְאָה וְלֶהָבָה, וְאָכְלָה
בַּעֲלֵי רָמוֹת. וְאָמַרְתִּי בְנַפְשִׁי קוּם כִּי זֶה הַיּוֹם לְבַטֵּל
בִּקּוּר הַפְּנֵקֶס בְּפִשְׁפּוּשׁ מַעֲשִׂים. וְהַיָּמִים הָאֵלֶּה
נִזְכָּרִים וְנַעֲשִׂים בִּתְשׁוּבָה וּתְפִלָּה וּצְדָקָה. לְמַעַן
יָצִיץ מֵחֲרַכָּהּ שֶׁכֵּן אֶת־דַּכָּא, וִיבַטֵּל מִמֶּנִּי כָּל־עָקָה
וְגַם כָּל־חֳלִי וְכָל־מַכָּה. וּמַחֲשַׁבְתִּי הַטּוֹבָה יְצָרֵף
לְמַעֲשֶׂה וְיַחְשְׁבֶהָ לִי צְדָקָה. וְיַגְבִּיהֶךָ לְמַעֲלָה רָמָה.
לְמַעֲלָה מִמַּלְאֲכֵי אֵיּוֹמָה: וְאַתָּה תִּשָּׂא בַעֲדִי רִנָּה
וּתְפִלָּה לְעֹלֵת כָּל־עֹלָה וְנוֹרָא עֲלִילָה. שִׁירִים
וְיַגְבִּיהַ מַזָּלִי לְמַעְלָה עַד־עוֹלָם סֶלָה. וְיַהֲפוֹךְ אָכְלִי
לְשָׂשׂוֹן וְצָהֳלָה. וִיבָרְכֵנִי בְּכָל־מִינֵי בְרָכָה וְהַצְלָחָה
וְטוֹבָה וְחַיִּים וְשִׂמְחָה. וִינַחֲמֵנִי בְּנֶחָמַת צִיּוֹן
וִירוּשָׁלָיִם: וְאַתָּה תָנוּחַ וְתַעֲמֹד לְגֹרָלְךָ לְקֵץ הַיָּמִין
אָמֵן:

———

All-merciful Father! grant me help and strength to carry out this determination. Give me a firm mind, that I may not waver. Remove from before me vice and temptation. Grant that my whole life be devoted to serve Thee with a perfect heart, and to revere thy great name. Deign that I may quit my earthly abode with a good name, followed by pious actions, and accompanied by humane and benevolent deeds. Grant that the pious spirit of my [father] [mother] may approach Thy glorious throne, and invoke Thy tender mercy on [him] [her], on me and on all that belong to me. May the pious deeds which [he] [she] performed, whilst alive, appear before Thy heavenly seat, and be accepted as the sweet savour of the frankincense. Fountain of mercy! give ear to [his] [her] prayers, in which [he] [she] beseeches Thy sacred name to bestow on [his] [her] descendants a long, blessed and happy life. [Beloved father] [affectionate mother], lift up thy voice to Him who is tremendous in work, that He may render me truly happy, and change my mourning into joy and gladness; that He may shower down upon me His heavenly blessings, and cause me to behold the consolation of Zion, His glorious residence, and of Jerusalem, His holy city, at the time when He will resuscitate all those who sleep in dust, and who wait for the day of everlasting felicity and glory. Amen.

ON VISITING THE GRAVE OF A FATHER.

שָׁלוֹם עָלֶיךָ אֲדוֹנִי אָבִי וּמוֹרִי, הוֹד זִיוִי וַהֲדָרִי,

בְּשָׁלוֹם יָנוּחוּ עַצְמוֹתֶיךָ בַּקֶּבֶר בָּעוֹלָם הַזֶּה, וְנִשְׁמָתְךָ

הוֹבְאָה לְחַיֵּי עַד לָעוֹלָם הַבָּא: וְיָדַעְתִּי כִּי שָׁלוֹם

אָהֳלֶךָ, וּמַעְלָה מַעְלָה עָלְתָה נִשְׁמָתְךָ, יוֹשֶׁבֶת

בְּסֵתֶר עֶלְיוֹן, וּבְצֵל שַׁדַּי תִּתְלוֹנָן: אַךְ אָנִי, אַיֵּה

אֶמְצָא מָנוֹחַ וּבַמֶּה אֶתְנֶחֵם, כָּל־יָמֶיךָ בִּי נִטְפַּלְתָּ

וְכָל־מַחְסוֹרִי הָיָה לִי עַל־יָדֶךָ, תָּמִיד הֲטִיבוֹתִי לִי

מִטּוּבְךָ, גַּם בַּתּוֹרָה הָאָרֶץְתָּ אֶת־עֵינַי וְלַמִּצְוֹוֹת

הִדְרַכְתָּ פְּעָמַי, וּבַעֲבוֹדַת יְיָ חִזַּקְתָּ אֶת יָדַי, וּמֵדֶּרֶךְ

הָרַע מָנַעְתָּ אֶת־רַגְלָי: וְעַתָּה הָלַכְתָּ לְךָ מַנְהִיגִי,

וְנִשְׁאַרְתִּי אֲנִי לְבַדִּי, וְאֵין לִי עוֹד מְנַהֵל וְלֹא מוֹרֶה

דֵעָה: הָה צַדִּיק נֶאֱסָף, וּבְנוֹ נֶעֱזָב: עַל־כֵּן הַיּוֹם

יָצָאתִי וְלִמְקוֹם מְלוֹנְךָ בָּאתִי, וְאֶשְׁתַּטֵּחַ עַל־קִבְרֶךָ

וְאֶשָּׂא עֵינַי לֵאלֹהֵי מָרוֹם אֲשֶׁר לוֹ הַיְשׁוּעָה וּמִמֶּנּוּ

הַנֶּחָמָה, וְהוּא רַחוּם יוֹשִׁיעֵנִי, וּבְחַסְדּוֹ יִרְפָּאֵנִי:

וְגַם אַתָּה אָבִי תִּסְעָדֵנִי, וַעֲמָד־נָא וְהִתְפַּלֵּל בַּעֲדִי,

וּבַקֵּשׁ עָלַי רַחֲמִים כִּהָאֵל רֹכֵב שְׁחָקִים, עַד כִּי

ON VISITING THE GRAVE OF A FATHER.

Peace be unto thee, my honored father and instructor, my glory and my delight! May thy bones rest in the grave in peace, and thy spirit be brought up to everlasting life. My soul still clings to thee with filial love, duty and affection. The sacred bonds between me and thee are not severed. I know that peace is in thy tabernacle of clay, and that thy soul has soared heavenward to the angelic abode of blissfulness, under the protection of the Most High, and under the shadow of the Almighty. But, alas! I, where am I to find rest, and with what shall I comfort myself. Thy whole earthly existence has been devoted to my welfare, to my physical and mental improvement. All my wants depended on thee, thou hast enlightened mine eyes in the Divine Law: thou hast guarded my steps and strengthened my hands in the service of God, and hast refrained my feet from walking in the way of sinners. But my glory has gone from me; I am left alone, without a guide, without a teacher. Alas! the righteous is taken away, and his son is forsaken.

I do, therefore, approach this awful and holy spot, the shrine that contains thy sacred ashes, and with a contrite spirit do I lift up mine eyes to God on high, the God of salvation and consolation, to implore His infinite mercy, that He may deign to send me a true help, because of His unbounded compassion. And thou, soul of my departed, beatified father, do support me with thy fervent prayer and invoke upon me the mercy, the love of Him who rideth upon the heavens, so that my light may break forth as the

יִבָּקַע כַּשַּׁחַר אוֹרִי, וַאֲרוּכָתִי מְהֵרָה תַצְמִיחַ: אָנָּא
יְיָ רִבּוֹן הָעוֹלָמִים. רְפָאֵנִי יְיָ וְאֵרָפֵא, הוֹשִׁיעֵנִי
וְאִוָּשֵׁעַ, עֲשֵׂה עִמִּי חֶסֶד לְמַעַן שְׁמֶךָ, אָנָּא תְנַחֲמֵנִי
וְאַל־תַּעַזְבֵנִי וְתִהְיֶה הַשְׁגָּחָתְךָ עָלַי תָּמִיד לְטוֹבָה,
וְתַצְלִיחַ אוֹתִי בְּכָל־עִנְיָנַי, וְתֵן רֶוַח וּבְרָכָה כְּמַעֲשֵׂי
יָדַי, וְהָאֵר עֵינַי בְּמִצְוֹתֶיךָ, וְדַבֵּק לִבִּי בְּתוֹרָתֶךָ, וְאַל־
תַשְׁלֶט־בִּי יֵצֶר הָרָע שֶׁלֹּא אָבוֹא לִידֵי חֵטְא, וְתִטַּע
בְּלִבִּי עֵצוֹת טוֹבוֹת, וְהָפֵר כָּל־עֲצַת רָעִים מֵעָלַי
וְהַצִּלֵנִי מִדִּין קָשֶׁה וּמִבַּעַל דִּין קָשֶׁה וּמֵעַז פָּנִים
וּמֵאָדָם רַע וּמֵחָבֵר רַע וּמִשָּׁכֵן רַע וּמִמִּקְרֶה רַע
וּמִכָּל־שָׁעוֹת רָעוֹת הַמִּתְרַגְּשׁוֹת לָבוֹא לָעוֹלָם, וּתְמַלֵּא
מִסְפַּר יָמַי בְּשָׁלוֹם וּבְמִיתָה טוֹבָה, וִיהִי יוֹם מִיתָתִי
כְּיוֹם לֵדָתִי, שֶׁלֹּא יִמָּצֵא בִּי שׁוּם חֵטְא
וְעָוֹן וְאַשְׁמָה וָרֶשַׁע, וְתָנוּחַ נַפְשִׁי בִּצְרוֹר
הַחַיִּים וְנַקֵּנִי בְּיוֹם הַדִּין וְצַדְּקֵנִי בַּמִּשְׁפָּט: אָנָּא
יְיָ תִּשְׁמַע קוֹל תְּפִלָּתִי, וְתַעֲשֶׂה אֶת־שְׁאֵלָתִי וּבַקָּשָׁתִי
בְּרַחֲמֶיךָ הָרַבִּים, אָמֵן:

morning star, and that my health may spring forth speedily.

I beseech Thee, Sovereign of the Universe! Heal me, and I shall be healed. Save me, and I shall be saved. Deal with me bountifully, for the sake of Thy name. I pray Thee, do comfort me, and forsake me not. May Thy Divine Providence be continually watching over me for my good. Prosper all my occupations, and bestow Thy paternal blessings on all the works of my hands. Deign to enlighten mine eyes in Thy commandments, and attach my heart unto Thy law. Let evil imagination have no dominion over me; may I neither fall into the power of sin, nor be allured by temptation. Teach me to conquer the one and to resist the other. Father in Heaven! imbue my heart with salutary counsels, and frustrate all evil designs against me. Rescue me from a bad man, from a severe judge and an implacable accuser, from a hardened and bold foe, from seducers, from evil associates, from wicked neighbors, from mishaps, and from disastrous occurrences which threaten to befall us in this transient world. Deign that the number of my years may be fulfilled in happiness and ease. May the day of my death be as the day of my birth: free from sin, and unstained by iniquities, guilt and ungodliness. Grant that my soul may be treasured up in the treasures of everlasting life. Cleanse me in the day of retribution, and justify me in Thy judgment. I beseech Thee, O Eternal, hear the voice of my prayer, and grant my request and supplication for the sake of Thine infinite mercy. Amen.

וְגַם אַתָּה אָבִי מוֹרִי, אֲשֶׁר אַתָּה מוֹרָשֵׁי לְבָבִי
יְמַלֵּא יְיָ כָּל־מִשְׁאֲלוֹתֶיךָ, לְהַעֲלוֹת נִשְׁמָתְךָ בְּחֻפָּצֶךָ,
וְתִשְׁכֹּן בְּצֵל עֵדֶן אֵצֶל הָאָבוֹת הַקְּדוֹשִׁים הַיְשָׁרִים
וְהַתְּמִימִים וְהַטְּהוֹרִים, וְתִזְכֶּה לַעֲמוֹד לִתְחִיָּה,
לְגוֹרָלְךָ הַנָּעִים בְּקֵץ הַיָּמִים, אָמֵן:

ON THE GRAVE OF A MOTHER.

שָׁלוֹם לָךְ אִמִּי מוֹרָתִי ׳ אֲשֶׁר טִפַּחַתְּ וְרִבִּית
אוֹתִי ׳ וְנִצְטַעַרְתְּ עָלַי בְּלִי שִׁעוּר כְּפֵאָה וּכְבִכּוּרִים
וְכָרָאָיוֹן ׳ וְנִטְפַּלְתְּ בִּי כָּל־יָמַיִךְ ׳ וְכָל־מַחְסוֹרִי הָיָה
לִי מִיָּדֶיךְ : וְעַתָּה מִיּוֹם אֲשֶׁר הָלַכְתְּ בְּדֶרֶךְ כָּל־
הָאָרֶץ לֹא נִשְׁאֲרָה לִי אוֹמֶנֶת כָּמוֹךְ ׳ כִּי בְכָל־עֵת
הֵכַנְתְּ אֶרֶץ־טוֹבָתִי : וּבִרְאוֹתִי אָרְחִי וָזוֹ צָרָתִי
הָלַכְתִּי לְשָׂדֶה בוֹכִים ׳ עַד שֶׁבָּאתִי אֶל־בֵּית אִמִּי
וּלְחֶדֶר הוֹרָתִי ׳ וְהִנֵּה הִיא לוּטָה בַּשִּׂמְלָה ׳ וְרוּחָהּ
עָלְתָה לְמַעְלָה. וְאָמַרְתִּי, שָׁלוֹם לָךְ וְשָׁלוֹם
לִמְנוּחָתֵךְ וְשָׁלוֹם לְנִשְׁמָתֵךְ ׳ מִנָּשִׁים בָּאֹהֶל תְּבֹרָךְ,
וְתָמִיד יֹאמַר עָלַיִךְ, קוּמִי אוֹרִי כִּי בָא אוֹרֵךְ ׳
וּכְבוֹד יְיָ עָלַיִךְ יִזְרָח: וְלִי אֲנִי עַבְדֵּךְ ׳ יַהֲמוּ־נָא

Thou also, spirit of my departed father, whose dear memory is engraved in the innermost chambers of my heart, may the Eternal fulfil thy desires. May thy soul soar up to the throne of mercy, to be seated next to our godly, pious, beatified, perfect and upright ancestors, until thine ashes are resusciated to everlasting life, and enjoy heavenly bliss allotted to thee at the end of the days. Amen.

ON THE GRAVE OF A MOTHER.

Peace unto thy beatified and pious soul, beloved and affectionate mother, who hast given me birth, and who hast reared me. Thou, who hast loved, fostered and cherished me, and who hast endured much suffering for me all the days of thy existence. Thou, whose maternal care has been unceasingly devoted to my happiness, whose eye so ardently watched over my physical and mental development. But, alas! since thou didst go the way of all flesh, I find nowhere a guide like unto thee. I therefore have strengthened myself on my way, and proceeded to the field of weeping, until I came to the house of my mother, and to the chamber of her who bore me. And lo! there I behold thine earthly remains, wrapt in the sleep of death, whilst thy soul has soared heavenwards, and I exclaim: peace be unto thy soul, and may thy repose be in glory, thou blessed of women! May continually be verified in thee the promise, Arise, shine, for thy light is come, and the glory of the Eternal is risen upon thee.

עָלַי רַחֲמֶיךָ ׳ לְהִתְפַּלֵּל בַּעֲדִי אֶל־יְיָ ׳ שֶׁיִּשְׁמַע קוֹל

תַּחֲנוּנַי ׳ כְּאָמְרִי , אָנָּא נוֹרָה וְקָדוֹשׁ תַּרְבֶּה

מְחִילָתֶךָ, פְּשָׁעַי לִסְלוֹחַ תִּגַּלְגֵּל מִדּוֹתֶיךָ ׳ יְחָנֵּנִי

מִיּוֹמַיִם בְּרַחֲמָיו עוֹשֶׂה שָׁלוֹם בִּמְרוֹמָיו ׳ וְיַסְפִּיק לִי

מִשָּׁמָיו בָּר וְלֶחֶם וּמָזוֹן בְּרַחֲמָיו ׳ וְאֶל־דִּמְעָתִי אַל־

יֶחֱרַשׁ, בְּקָרְאִי מִן־הַמֵּצַר בְּעֹנִי וָרָשׁ: יְחָנֵּנִי וְיֹאמַר

פְּדָעֵהוּ מֵרֶדֶת שַׁחַת ׳ וְלֹא יֶחְסַר לַחְמוֹ וְלֹא יָמוּת

לַשַּׁחַת ׳ וִיזַכֵּנִי לִרְאוֹת בָּנִים וּבְנֵי בָנִים בַּתּוֹרָה

וּבְמִצְווֹת עוֹסְקִים ׳ וְיִהְיוּ בַּעֲלֵי מִצְווֹת וְשֵׁם טוֹב

וְצַדִּיקִים ׳ וּמִכָּל־עָוֹן וְאַשְׁמָה מְנֻקִּים: וְאַתְּ נִשְׁמָתֵךְ

תִּשְׁכֹּון בְּצֵל עֲצֵי עֵדֶן אֵצֶל הָאִמָּהוֹת הַיְשָׁרוֹת

הַקְּדוֹשׁוֹת וְהַטְּהֹרוֹת: וְתִזְכִּי לַעֲמֹד לִתְחִיָּה עִם־

שְׁאָר נָשִׁים שֶׁאֲנָבוֹת וַחֲסִידִים וַחֲסִידוֹת בְּנוֹת

עֲלֶיהָ ׳ וְתַעַמְדִי לְגֹרָלֵךְ לְקֵץ הַיָּמִין ׳ כֵּן יַעֲשֶׂה הָאֵל

יְיָ, אָמֵן:

But I, thy servant, turn unto thee, that thou mayest invoke upon thy [son] [daughter] the tender mercies of God, that He may vouchsafe to hear the voice of my supplication, when I say, O Thou awfully sublime and holy God! extend Thy forgiveness, pardon my transgressions, and let Thine ineffable attributes prevail! May He who establishes peace in His high heavens be gracious unto us, as in time of old. May He from His celestial seat grant me daily food and sustenance, and not be silent unto my tears, when in distress I call upon the Eternal as a poor and needy one. May He be gracious unto me and bid His benign messengers: "Redeem him from going down into the grave. May his bread not fail, nor should he see corruption." Grant that I may be worthy to behold children and children's children attached and devoted to Thy sacred laws, to perform, Thy commandments, to walk in the path of uprightness, and be adorned with the crown of a good name free from sin and pure from guilt.

May thy pious soul rest in calm and quietude in the garden of Eden, in the circle of the pious and righteous mothers in Israel. Mayest thou be deemed worthy to rise to everlasting life, in fellowship with all those pious, virtuous and godly daughters, to stand for thy lot at the end of the days. May God please to do so. Amen.

ON THE GRAVE OF A WIFE.

One married a second time, must not visit the grave of his first wife.

נֶפֶשׁ טְהוֹרָה עָלִית לְרוּם חֶבְיוֹן נַפְשֵׁךְ בְּטוּב

תָּלִין וּמְדוֹרֵךְ עִם־דַהַתְּמִימוֹת שָׂרָה רִבְקָה רָחֵל

וְלֵאָה: אִשָּׁה כְּשֵׁרָה בַּנָּשִׁים מְאֻשָּׁרָה נְקִיָּה

וּטְהוֹרָה אֱלֹהִים יְיָ נָאְזָר בִּגְבוּרָה יָשִׂים חֶלְקָהּ

עִם־שָׂרָה: אִשָּׁה כְּשֵׁרָה. בַּנָּשִׁים חֲשׁוּקָה נֵר

שַׁבָּת הִדְלִיקָה כְּחָקָהּ הָאֵל הַנִּקְדָּשׁ בִּצְדָקָהּ

יָשִׂים חֶלְקָהּ עִם־רִבְקָה: אִשָּׁה כְּשֵׁרָה בַּנָּשִׁים

נָאָה חַלָּתָהּ קָצְצָה בְּמִלּוּאָהּ. הָאֵל אֲשֶׁר גָּאָה

נָאָה יָשִׂים חֶלְקָהּ עִם־לֵאָה: הָאֵל חוֹמֵל וּמוֹחֵל

יִזְבָּר־לָהּ רַחֲמָיו עִם־כְּבוּדוֹת וּצְנוּעוֹת נַחֲלָתָהּ

תִּנְחָל, לִהְיוֹת מָנָתָהּ עִם־רָחֵל: אֵשֶׁת חַיִל עֲטֶרֶת

בַּעְלֵךְ מַלְאֲכֵי רַחֲמִים יִפְתְּחוּ לָךְ שַׁעֲרֵי עֵדֶן

וְתִתְעַדֵּן הַנְּשָׁמָה הַתְּמִימָה וְתִרְאֶה אוֹרָה מֵאֵל

נָאוֹר אֲשֶׁר מֵעֵין כָּל־חַי נֶעְלָמָה: וְאַתְּ כִּי נָסַעַתְּ

לַמְּנוּחוֹת בִּגְזֵרַת קַדִּישִׁין וּכְמַאֲמַר עִירִין וְעָזַבְתְּ

ON THE GRAVE OF A WIFE.

One married a second time, must not visit the grave of his first wife.

Pious, purified soul of my beloved wife! Thou didst soar up to the secret clouds, to the regions of peace, under the protection of the Most High. There thou abidest in felicity, whilst I am [*and thy descendants are] yet tarrying on earth. O thou truly faithful, affectionate and loving spirit, mayest thou now receive the reward for thy faithfulness in the circle of the pious and beatified mothers, and the God-fearing and virtuous daughters of Israel.

Most virtuous of wives! pure and spotless soul! Thou hast at all times been girded with the fear of God, animated with the enlightened spirit of our mother Sarah, actuated by the truly benevolent feelings of Rebecca, and adorned with the modest and virtuous sentiments of Rachel and Leah. Thou hast most cheerfully and most earnestly watched over my household, [to teach the sons, to instruct the daughters, and to precede them with thy pious example;] to cheer the hearts of the poor, to celebrate the sacred festivals, and to sanctify the sabbath. Thou hast changed my house into a temple, and my table into an altar. Thou hast watched over their sanctity. Mayest thou now enjoy the godly fruit of thine ardent zeal and pious efforts in the regions of uninterrupted happiness.

O may our merciful Father command His benign angels of peace to open unto thee the gates of Eden, to seat thee in the assembly of pure souls, and may

---

* A father of a family adds.

אוֹתָנוּ לַאֲנָחוֹת וּלְמִשְׁלַחַת גְּרִין · יְהִי נָא חַסְדְּךָ
עָלֵינוּ · לְהַמְשִׁיךְ בִּתְפִלָּתֵךְ חוּט שֶׁל־חֶסֶד עָלֵינוּ ·
אַחֲרֵי כִּי יָדַעַתְּ כִּי אָדָם אֵין צַדִּיק בָּאָרֶץ · אֲשֶׁר אֵין
כַּעֲסוֹ לִפְעָמִים יֶרֶץ לְהַקְדִּים לְרַחֲמִים פָּנִים זְעוּמִים .
וְאוּלַי הַכַּעַס חֵבִיא נַם אוֹתִי לִידֵי טָעוּת · לְתֵת
בְּעֶקְרֶת הַבַּיִת מִגְרָעַת · כְּהוֹנָאַת דְּבָרִים הַמְּבִיאִים
לִידֵי דְמָעוֹת · אוֹ בִּשְׁאָר גִּלְגּוּלֵי סִבּוֹת הַמְּבִיאִים
לִידֵי תִגְרָאוֹת · מְחַלְ־נָא סְלַח־נָא לִי הַהוֹנָאָה
וְאַל־תִּזְכְּרִי לִי שׁוּם חוֹבָא : וּמַהֵר יְקַדְּמוּנִי רַחֲמֶיךָ .
לַעֲמֹד בִּתְפִלָּה בִּשְׁבִילֵנוּ אֶת־פְּנֵי יְיָ אֱלֹהָיִךְ ·
הַמְחַיֶּה חַיִּים, אוֹמֵר וְעֹשֶׂה גּוֹזֵר וּמְקַיֵּם . שֶׁיִּגְדֹּר
הַפִּרְצָה הַפְּרוּצָה. וִיבַטֵּל כָּל־גְּזֵרָה הָרוּצָה. וְיִתֶּן־לָנוּ
חַיִּים אֲרוּכִים בְּכָבוֹד וּבְעשֶׁר וּבְמִלּוּי וְלֹא כְחֹסֶר. כְּדֵי
שֶׁאוּכַל לְפַרְנֵם זַרְעִי וּבְנֵי בֵאתִי . וּלְגַדְּלָם לַעֲבוֹדַת
הַשֵּׁם כַּאֲשֶׁר עִם־לְבָבִי וְדַעְתִּי . וְיִחְיוּ כָל־בְּנֵי בֵתִי
בְּשָׁלוֹם וּבְאַהֲוָה וּבְכָבוֹד וּבְהַצְלָחָה וּבְהַרְוָחָה :
תִּשְׂאִי בַעֲדִי רִנָּה וּתְפִלָּה . וְהַפְגִּיעִי שֶׁיַּצִּלֵנִי הָאֵל

thine eyes now feast on the radiant glory of the
Divine presence, which is hidden from the eyes of
frail mortals. Beloved and revered spirit! God, in
His inscrutable wisdom, has pleased to terminate
thine earthly pilgrimage, to summon thee to regions
of everlasting repose, whilst I am yet ordained to
tarry in the valley of sorrow; be thou therefore my
guide. Approach the throne of mercy, and implore
upon me grace, that I may not stumble on my dismal
intricate and rugged path. Remember not, when in
an unheeded moment of impetuosity or unguarded
passion, my mouth might have uttered harsh expressions and words of unkindness, which caused
thee grief, sorrow and trouble. O, do pardon and
forgive me! May thine affection, thy love, thy sympathy, which have not ceased with thy death, be my
polar star, to lead me to the land of life and of
blissfulness, to illumine my gloomy and dismal nights,
and to protect me from danger, from trouble and
mishaps.

May thy pure soul unite with me in prayer before
the Dispenser of all events, to guard me from affliction, grief and sickness, and to grant unto me and
all that belong to me, a long and happy life: a life of
honor, of plenty; free from care [*so that I may
maintain my children and my household, and train
them in the service of His sacred name, according to
the true and unfeigned desire of my heart.] May
peace, blessing, ease, honor, plenty and glory be the
portion of my inheritance. Lift up thy voice in
prayer and supplication to the Father of mercy; im-

* A father of a family adds.

מִכָּל־זַעַם וְצָרָה. וַיְחַיֵּנִי לְאֹרֶךְ יָמִים וְשָׁנִים. וִימַלֵּא

יָמַי בַּטּוֹב וּשְׁנוֹתַי בַּנְּעִימִים. וְיִהְיוּ כָל־זַרְעִי וְזֶרַע

זַרְעִי חֲסִידִים וּתְמִימִים . וְלֹא יִמָּצֵא בָהֶם שׁוּם שֶׁמֶץ

וְדֹפִי וּפְגָמִים . וְלֹא יִצְטָרְכוּ לִבְנֵי אָדָם . וְלֹא יָצִיפוּ

לְשׁוּלְחָן אֲחֵרִים. וְלֹא יוּכְנָעוּ תַּחַת זָרִים: קוּם קְרָא

אֶל־אֱלֹהֶיךָ אַל־תְּאַחֲרִי . הִתְפַּלְלִי בַּעֲדֵינוּ וְאֶל־אֵל

שַׁחֲרִי : וְהוּא רַחוּם יְמַלֵּא בַקָּשָׁתֵךְ עֲבוּרֵנוּ .

בִּזְכוּתֵךְ וּבִזְכוּת כָּל־הַצַּדִּיקִים אֲבוֹתֵינוּ : וְאֵת

אֲהוּבָתִי גוּפֵךְ יָנוּחַ בְּהַשְׁקֵט וְשָׁלוֹם . וְנִשְׁמָתֵךְ

תֶּחֱזֶה בְשַׁלְוָה בַּמָּרוֹם אָמֵן סֶלָה :

PRAYER FOR A WIDOW ON THE GRAVE
OF HER HUSBAND.

One married a second time must not visit the grave of her first
husband.

שָׁלוֹם עָלֶיךָ אַתָּה אִישִׁי וּבַעֲלִי . אֲשֶׁר הָיִיתָ בִּנְיַן

בֵּיתִי וְשִׂמְחַת אָהֳלִי. הָיִיתָ מֵאִיר מַאֲפֵלִי . וּמְנַהֵר

plore His sacred name, that He may deliver us from
trouble and affliction, and that I and all who belong
to me may fulfil our years in happiness and content,
even to a good old age. [Merciful Father! grant
that my descendants may be good, virtuous, upright
and pious, free from sin and blemish, so that they
may never defile or desecrate Thy great name. Cause
their light to break forth as the morning, and may
their health speedily spring forth. Gracious Father!
Deign that I may train them in, and lead them to
the glorification of Thy sacred name and holy service; do not subject them to the gifts of the sons of
men, nor suffer that they stay their hunger by that
reached to them at the tables of strangers. Incline
their hearts to study and to search Thy sacred law,
and guard them against malice, envy, and discord.]
Arise, call upon thy God! tarry not, invoke his
mercy, that He may listen to our supplication, for
the sake of the merit of our pious forefathers, and of
all the godly and virtuous ones who sleep in the
dust.

Purest of souls, thou my beloved! May thine
ashes rest in ease and tranquillity. Abide thou in
everlasting and uninterrupted felicity, and rise at the
appointed time, when the Almighty will awaken thee
to constant glory and perpetual life. Amen.

PRAYER FOR A WIDOW ON THE GRAVE OF HER HUSBAND.

One married to another must not visit the grave of her first husband.

Peace be unto thee, thou spirit of my beatified
husband! Thou who hast been the prop of my house,
and the delight of my dwelling. Thou who hast

מַחֲשַׁכֵּי הָיִיתָ לִי עֲטֶרֶת צְבִי. וּרְפֻאוֹת מַכְאוֹבִי:

וְעַתָּה שִׁמְשִׁי שָׁקְעָה: וְנִשְׁעַרְתִּי כָדַד וְגַלְמוּדָה.

בְּבוֹאִי לְבֵיתִי וְאֶפְנֶה כֹּה וָכֹה וְאֶרְאֶה כִּי אֵין אִישׁ.

וָאֹמַר אַיֶּכָּה: אֵיכָה עֲזַבְתַּנִי עֲזוּבָה וּשְׁבוּחָה אִשָּׁה

עֲצוּבַת רוּחַ. בָּכֹה אֶבְכֶּה וְדִמְעָתִי עַל־לֶחֱיִי. אֵין

לִי מְנַחֵם וְלֹא מֵשִׁיב יְגוֹנִי. וָאָבֹא הַיּוֹם אֶל־הָעַיִן

כְּבַת עֵינִי. אֶל־נִקְרַת צוּר מְנוּחַת הֲדַר שְׁשׁוֹנִי.

וּבִקַּשְׁתִּיו וְלֹא מְצָאתִיו: אַךְ מִן־הַמֵּצַר קְרָאתִיו:

וַאֹמַר, שָׁלוֹם לָךְ וּלְנִשְׁמָתָךְ הַטְּהוֹרָה. בְּצֵל עֲנַן

כָּבוֹד תִּהְיֶה שְׁמוּרָה: לָעַד וּלְנֶצַח תִּהְיֶה לְטוֹב

זְכוּרָה: וְהִנֵּה נָא רָאֹה תִרְאֶה וְזָכַרְתָּ אֶת־אֲמָתֶךָ.

וּרְאֵה עָנְיִי וְשִׁפְלוּתִי. וּנְמִיכַת רוּחִי וְצָרוֹתַי. עַל־

מִי נָטַשְׁתָּ מְעַט הַצֹּאן הָהֵנָּה. כִּכְשׁוֹת צֹאנְךָ וְצֹאנִי

אֲשֶׁר הַצַּבְתָּ לְבַדָּנָה: נָסַעְתָּ אַתָּה לִמְנוּחוֹת.

וְעֹזַבְתָּ אוֹתָנוּ לַאֲנָחוֹת: מִי יוֹרֶה דֵעָה וּמִי יָבִין

שְׁמוּעָה גְּמוּלֵי מֵחָלָב וְעַתִּיקֵי מִשָּׁדָיִם. מִי יוֹרֶה לָּנוּ

דַּרְכֵי אֱלֹהִים חַיִּים. מִי יַדְרִיכֵנוּ בִּנְתִיב יֹשֶׁר. וּמִי

יוֹרֶה לָּנוּ שְׁעַת הַכֹּשֶׁר: וְעַל־מִי הִבְטַחְתָּ אַלְמָנָתֶךָ.

וּמִי יִבְנֶה בִּנְיַן בֵּיתֶךָ: וְאִם תִּדְרְמֶה מִיתַת אִשָּׁה

enlightened my darkness and cheered my gloominess. Thou, the crown of my glory, and the remedy of my affliction. But, alas! now my sun has gone down, and I, a bereaved widow, am left alone and destitute. My brightness disappeared, and my delight vanished. Alas! when I enter my house, when I look this way and that way and perceive thee not, I exclaim in the anguish of my heart, Where art thou? Wherefore hast thou forsaken me, the grieved of spirit? Who will console me, who will heal my affliction, and who will stay the tears on my cheeks? I come to-day to the valley of the fountain of tears; to the cleft of the rock of the resting place of my delight and joy. I sought him and found him not; then I called out from distress, Peace be unto thee, and to thy purified soul. Mayest thou rest in, and be protected under the shadow of the Divine Glory, and ever be remembered for good.

I beseech Thee, O God! look on the affliction of Thy handmaid; behold my grief, my contrition, my crushed spirit, my troubled mind and my great disquietude. *[Behold, with whom hast thou left these sheep,—mine and thine, lambs which thou hast left to themselves! Thou didst go to rest, but us thou hast left to sorrow. Who shall teach them knowledge, who make them that are weaned from the milk understand the ways of the living God and the spirit of our inherited faith? Who will guide us in the path of rectitude, and who will teach us the right and proper use of time?] To whom hast thou entrusted thy sorrowful widow? Verily, if the death

---

*A Mother of a young family adds.

עַל־בַּעֲלָהּ כְּחָרְבָּן הַבַּיִת בְּיָמָיו. הִנֵּה תִדְמֶה מִיתַת

הַבַּעַל עַל־אִשְׁתּוֹ כְּאִלּוּ נֶחֱרַב הָעוֹלָם וּמְרוֹמָיו . עַל

כֵּן רַחֵם עַל־פְּלֵטַת צֹאן יָדֶךָ . וַעֲמָד־נָא בִּתְפִלָּה

וּבְבַקָּשָׁה לִפְנֵי אֵל רָם וְנִשָּׂא אֲבִי יְתוֹמִים וְדַיַּן

אַלְמָנוֹת: שֶׁיְּכַפֵּר עַל־חַטֹּאתַי וְיִבְנֶה הֲרִיסוֹתַי ·

וְיָשִׂים צָרַי לְמַכְאוֹבִי · וִירַחֵם עָלַי וְעַל־טַפִּי אֲשֶׁר

תָּלוּ בִי · וִינַחֵם אוֹתִי וִירַפֵּא כְאֵבִי · וְיָסִיר כָּל־

מַחֲלָה וְכָל־נֶגַע מִקִּרְבִּי · וַיְשֵׁב בִּנְיַן בֵּיתִי הֶהָרוּס ·

וְלִרְעֵבִי לֶחֶם מָזוֹן וְצֵדָה יִפְרוֹס · וִינַדְּלֵם כְּעֵץ אֶרֶז

וּבְרוֹשׁ · וְיָאִיר מַאֲפֵלָנוּ כְּסַהַר וָחֶרֶס · וְיַשְׁאִיר לָנוּ

עָנָף וָשֹׁרֶשׁ · בָּנִים וּבְנֵי בָנִים · חֲכָמִים וּנְבוֹנִים ·

נְשׂוּאֵי פָנִים · עוֹסְקִים בַּתּוֹרָה וּבְמִצְוֹת כָּל־הַזְּמַנִּים ·

וּבַאֲרִיכֵי יָמִים וְשָׁנִים בְּעֹשֶׁר וְכָבוֹד עַל־מֵי מְנוּחוֹת

חוֹנִים: וְאַתָּה, נִשְׁמָתְךָ הָאֲהוּבָה · תָּמִיד יִזְכְּרֶנָּה

אֱלֹהִים לְטוֹבָה · וְגוּפְךָ יָנוּחַ פֹּה בִּמְנוּחָה, עַד כִּי־

תַעֲמֹד לִתְחִיָּה, לְשָׁשׂוֹן וּלְחֶדְוָה, אָמֵן:

of a wife to a husband has been compared to one
doomed to see the destruction of the glorious temple,
then the death of a husband to a wife surely re-
sembles the overthrow of the whole universe. Rise,
therefore, beloved of my soul; pray, supplicate and
implore the mercy of the Most High and Holy One,
the Father of the fatherless and the Judge of the
widows, to have mercy on the remnant of thy flock;
that He may deign to pardon my sins, and to support
my house that is broken down, to grant me a remedy
for my sufferings, and to look down from His celestial
abode with compassion on me, and on all that depend
on me. Heavenly Father! be Thou my comforter,
my healer; remove from me every disease and affliction, repair my ruin and provide for me and my
children our daily wants. Grant that they may
grow up like the cedars: that their roots may strike,
and their branches spread. May their remotest
posterity be wise, understanding, honored, attached
to Thy sacred law, and devoted to piety and virtue,
and may they spend long years in riches, honor and
ease.

Grant me Thy paternal aid; strengthen me in the
fulfilment of my arduous task, for it is Thou who
protectest the weak, and raisest the drooping spirits
of the fatherless, and never despisest the prayers of
widows.

And thou, heavenly soul of my beatified husband!
May God remember thee for good. May thy sacred
ashes repose in peace, until thou art awakened to
everlasting life, and to uninterrupted bliss, joy and
gladness. Amen.

PRAYER ON VISITING THE GRAVE OF
GROWN-UP CHILDREN.

שָׁלוֹם עָלַיִךְ נִשְׁמָה יְחִידָה, אֲשֶׁר הָיִית מְחַיָּה

גּוּף אָדָם אֲשֶׁר נַפְשִׁי לוֹ כָּמַהּ, מוֹצָא מֵעַי וִיוֹצֵא

חֲלָצַי אֲשֶׁר נָתַן לִי אֱלֹהִים בָּוֶּה עַל־פְּנֵי תֵבֵל

אַרְצוֹ כַּאֲשֶׁר יָשַׁר בְּעֵינָיו ּ בִּרְצוֹנוֹ נָתַן וּבִרְצוֹנוֹ

נָטָל : חָבִיב הָיָה עָלַי דִּבּוּרוֹ ּ תֵּאַוַּה נַפְשִׁי לִשְׁמוֹ

וּלְזִכְרוֹ ּ הוֹדִי חָמַק עָבָר, נִגְלָה וְנִכְסָה נִרְאָה

וְנִסְתָּר, קְרָאתִיו וְלֹא עָנָנִי בַּקְשְׁתִּיהוּ וְלֹא מְצָאתִיהוּ:

וַאֲנִי לֹא יָדַעְתִּי כַּכְּשֵׁי דִי רַחֲמָנָא וְרָזוֹהִי ּ אִם הָיָה

מַתָּנָה עַל־מְנָת לְהַחֲזִירָהּ בִּזְמַנָּהּ ּ אוֹ אִם־עֲוֹנֵינוּ

עָנוּ בָנוּ לְאֵיזוֹ סִיבָּה מֵהָעֲוֹנוֹת שֶׁחִיַּבְתִּי עֲלֵיהֶן

לְקַבֵּל הַפֻּרְעָנוּת: בֵּין כָּךְ וּבֵין כָּךְ לֹא זָכִיתִי לְגַדְּלוֹ

יוֹתֵר, וְאַף כִּי אָמַרְתִּי אַחֲרֵי מוֹתִי אֵלֶּה כְתָמָר

אֶחֱזֶה בְּסַנְסִנָּיו, נִפְרְדוּ נַפְרְצוּ עָלָיו בִּגְזֵרַת אֲדוֹנָיו,

וְאֵלְכָה לִי שְׂדֵה בוֹכִים, אֶל־הַסֶּלַע וְאֶל־הַבּוֹכִים,

וְאֶתְפַּלְּלָה אֶל־אֵל עַל־נִשְׁמָתוֹ, יַעֲלֶנָּה אֶל־מְכוֹן

שִׁבְתּוֹ, וְיַסְתִּירֶנָּה בְּסֵתֶר עֶלְיוֹן יָרוּם חֶבְיוֹן: וְאַתְּ

נִשְׁמָה עִמְדִי־נָא בִּתְפִלָּה וּבַקָּשָׁה לִפְנֵי אֵל רָם

PRAYER ON VISITING THE GRAVE OF GROWN-UP CHILDREN.

Peace be unto thee, thou pure soul! Thou, my delight, my longing, with whom God had favored me on this terrestrial world. Thou hast been entrusted to me by His infinite kindness, and in His unsearchable wisdom He deemed proper to deprive me of thee. Blessed be His sacred name. O how beloved were thy words to me. Thy name, thy remembrance, were the delight of my soul. But, alas! my beloved has withdrawn from me. He appeared and vanished; I called him, but he gave me no answer; I sought him, but found him not. I, short-sighted mortal, dare not penetrate into the Divine secret. I cannot fathom the reason of thy untimely departure. Hast thou only been entrusted to me for a certain time, or have my sins been the cause of thy early death and my heavy affliction? Alas! either way I was not permitted to train and rear thee, beloved child. Thou didst come forth like a flower; thou didst blossom in the morning, thou didst promise precious fruits; but how untimely, how early in life hast thou been blasted by a scorching sun, and crushed by a temptuous storm, like a flower that is cut down in the morning, withered and scattered. I, a sadly bereaved [father] [mother], come therefore to the valley of weeping, to pray to God that He may receive thy soul in His heavenly seat, and to protect it in His sublime and secret place.

Thou most pure and heavenly soul! Rise and appear with prayer and supplication before the Most

וְנִשָּׂא, שֶׁיְּכַפֵּר וְיִסְלַח לַעֲוֹנוֹת וְלַפְּשָׁעִים וְלַמַּעֲשִׂים
הָרָעִים שֶׁחָטָאתִי וְשֶׁעָוִיתִי וְשֶׁפָּשַׁעְתִּי וְשֶׁהֲרֵעוֹתִי
וִינַהֲלֵנִי עַל־מֵי מְנוּחוֹת בְּנַחַת וְשׁוּבָה עַד־זִקְנָה
וְשֵׂיבָה, וְיִשְׁמֹר אוֹתִי וּשְׁאָר זַרְעִי מִן־כִּלָּיוֹן וְחֻרְבָּן
עוֹד כָּל־יְמֵי הָאָרֶץ, וּמִמִּיתָה שֶׁלֹּא בִזְמַנָּהּ, גַּם
מִכָּל־חֳלִי וְכָל־מַכָּה· וְיִשְׁמֹר צֵאתִי וּבֹאִי לְחַיִּים
וּלְשָׁלוֹם מֵעַתָּה וְעַד עוֹלָם: וְאַתְּ לְכִי לַקֵּץ וּתְנוּחִי
וְתַעֲמְדִי לְגֹרָלֵךְ לְקֵץ הַיָּמִין עִם כָּל־הַצַּדִּיקִים:
וְהוּא רַחוּם יְכַפֵּר עָוֹן, וְלֹא יַשְׁחִית, וְהִרְבָּה לְהָשִׁיב
אַפּוֹ, וְלֹא יָעִיר כָּל־חֲמָתוֹ, וּבְשָׁלְחוֹ אֶת אֵלִיָּה
הַנָּבִיא לְפָנַי בּוֹא הַיּוֹם הַגָּדוֹל וְהַנּוֹרָא· אֲשֶׁר יָבוֹא
לְהָשִׁיב לֵב בָּנִים עַל־אֲבוֹתָם וְלֵב־אָבוֹת עַל־בָּנִים,
אֲוַי גַּם לִי גַּם לָךְ יְנַחֵם, אָמֵן:

PRAYER ON VISITING THE GRAVE OF
INFANTS.

שָׁלוֹם עָלַיִךְ נְשָׁמָה טְהוֹרָה· אֲשֶׁר מַלְבֶּשֶׁת הָיִית
בְּגוּף זַרְעִי· וְלֹא יָצָאת לְעוֹלָם אֶלָּא בְּכֹחַ וְלֹא
בְּפֹעַל הִרְבִּית: וַאֲנַחְנוּ לֹא נֵדַע כְּבֹשֵׁי דִי רַחֲמָנָא
וְהַסְּבָּרָה· אִם־הֵם יִסּוּרִים שֶׁל־אַהֲבָה· אוֹ אִם־
עֲוֹנֵינוּ עָנוּ בָנוּ כִּי־בָא הוֹבָה: וְלֹא פִי יַרְשִׁיעֵנִי

High and exalted One, that He may deign to pardon and to forgive the sins and transgressions, and the evil deeds which I have committed. May He lead me in ease, comfort and quietude, even to an old and hoary age; may He ever guard me and the remainder of my children from irrevocable destruction, from untimely death, from every sickness and plague; and guard my going out and my coming in, with life and peace, from henceforth and for evermore. Beloved child! Go to thine end, and repose in peace, and rise for thy lot at the end of the days, with all the righteous ones. And He being merciful, forgiveth iniquity, and destroyeth not; yea, He frequently turneth away His anger, and awakeneth not all His wrath, and when He will send Elijah the prophet before the coming of the great and fearful day of the Eternal, to restore the heart of fathers to their children, and the heart of children to their fathers, then He will comfort both me and thee! Amen.

PRAYER ON VISITING THE GRAVE OF INFANTS.

Peace be unto thee, pure soul, once wrapt in the body of my beloved child! How transitory has thy earthly life been! Thy existence was more ideal than reality. We, frail mortals, dare not, cannot dive into the hidden wisdom of the unscrutable decree, to unravel the cause of thy early, untimely death. Is it merely as a trial of my implicit resignation, of my love to, and my faith in God, or is it because of my sins that testify against me? But let

לֵאמֹר מִפְּנֵי מָה מֵחוּ פָנֶיךָ בְּחַיֶּיךָ, קוּם וְהִצְטַדֵּק
לִפְנֵי אֱלֹהֶיךָ, וְאֵלֶּה הַצֹּאן מֶה־עָשׂוּ, אֲשֶׁר מֵעוֹלָמָם
יָצְאוּ וּפָרָשׁוּ? כִּי עַל־הַכֹּל יְיָ אֱלֹהֵינוּ אֲנַחְנוּ מוֹדִים
לָךְ ׀ וּמַצְדִּיקִים דִּינְךָ וּלְיִרְאָתְךָ אָנוּ חֲרֵדִים: וַאֲנִי
תְפִלָּה לְאֵל חַי ׀ שֶׁיַּעֲלֶה הַנְּשָׁמָה הַטְּהוֹרָה ׀ אֶל־
מוּל־פְּנֵי שְׁכִינָתוֹ לְהָאִירָה ׀ וְיִשְׁתַּעֲשַׁע בָּהּ שַׁעֲשׁוּעִים
וַאֲהָבִים וְיַעֲלֶהָ בְּמַעֲלַת הַכְּרוּבִים: וְאַתָּה זַרְעִי
אֲשֶׁר הָיִיתָ מַתָּנָה בְּיָדִי לְפִי שָׁעָה ׀ עֲמֹד בִּתְפִלָּה
וּבְבַקָּשָׁה לִפְנֵי מַאֲזִין שַׁוְעָהּ ׀ וִיכַפֵּר עֲוֹנִי אֲשֶׁר־
גָּרְמוּ לְקִיחָתְךָ מִמֶּנִּי וְאַל־יְבַעֲתוּנִי שְׁבָטוֹ וְאֵימָתוֹ ׀
וִימַלֵּא יָמַי בַּטּוֹב וּשְׁנוֹתַי בַּנְּעִימִים ׀ אַךְ טוֹב וָחֶסֶד
יִרְדְּפוּנִי כָּל־יְמֵי חַיָּי וְשַׁבְתִּי בְּבֵית־יְיָ לְאֹרֶךְ יָמִים ׀
וְיַצֵּל אוֹתִי וּשְׁאָר זַרְעִי מִמִּיתָה מְשֻׁכֶּלֶת ׀ וּמִכָּל־
מַחֲלָה וּבֶהָלֵת ׀ וּמִכָּל־צָרָה וְצוּקָה ׀ וּבוּקָה מְבוּקָה
וּמְבֻלָּקָה ׀ וְיִמְחַל עֲוֹנִי וּזְדוֹנִי ׀ וְאַל־יוֹסִיף לְיַסְּרֵנִי:
וְרַחֲמָנָא דִּי־רָחֵם עַל־אֲבָהָתָנָא צַדִּיקַיָּא ׀ יַעֵל יָתָךְ
לְגַן עֵדֶן לְהִשְׁתַּעֲשַׁע בַּהֲדֵי צַדִּיקַיָּא ׀ וְהַעֲדָרָךְ יְהֵא
כַפָּרָא עֲלָנָא וְעַל כָּל־אַנְשֵׁי כְיתָנָא ׀ וָקֳדָם מָרֵא
עָלְמָא לֶהֱוֵא כְקָרְבָּן דִּי מִתְקַבַּל בְּרַעֲוָא ׀ וְלָא יוֹסִיף
עוֹד לְדַאֲבָה ׀ וְיִמְחַל חוֹבָנָא וְיִתֵּן־לָנָא בְּנִין דִּכְרִין

not my own mouth pronounce me guilty, saying:
Wherefore have thy children died during thy life?
I will rise and justify myself before God. For, as
for these lambs, what have they done to terminate
their earthly existence? Yet for all this do we render
our thanks unto Thee, and declare the justice of
Thy sentence, and tremble at Thy reverence. And
Thou, Eternal God of my life! hearken unto my
prayer, and may the pure soul of my beloved child
rise and shine in the presence of Thy Divine glory,
and in the assembly of the cherubim!

Thou, my child, who hast been entrusted to me but
for a moment, rise with thy supplication before Him
who hearkens to prayer, that He may deign to
pardon my sins, the cause of thy early death! May
His rod and dread not terrify me; may my days be
fulfilled in happiness, and my years in pleasantness!
May naught but happiness and tender mercy attend
me all the days of my life, so that I may dwell in the
house of the Eternal in length of days. May He in
His mercy deliver me and the remnant of my children
from death and barrenness, from disease and dejec-
tion, from trouble and distress, and from want and
misery. May the Most Merciful, who bestoweth
His infinite compassion on our righteous forefathers,
lead thee, beloved soul, into the garden of Eden:
there to delight in the fellowship of the righteous.
May thy untimely death be considered as an offering
for, and an expiation of my sins and of those of my
household, so that He may not continue to afflict
me. Grant to bless me with good children, who may
enjoy good health, and delight in Thy sacred law.

דִּי יְחֵיוֹן · וִיהוֹן עָסְקִין בְּאוֹרַיְתָא קַדִּישְׁתָּא · וְיַעֲדָא
מִנָּן וּמִן־כָּל־עַמֵּהּ בֵּית יִשְׂרָאֵל צָרָה וְיָגוֹן וַאֲנָחָה
וְכָל־מַרְעִין בִּישִׁין, אָמֵן:

———

PRAYER ON VISITING THE BURIAL GROUND ON THE DAY BEFORE NEW YEAR (ערב ראש השנה) AND ON THE DAY BEFORE YOM KIPPUR.

יְהִי רָצוֹן לְפָנֶיךָ יְיָ אֱלֹהֵי הָרַחֲמִים וְהַסְּלִיחוֹת,
מֶלֶךְ עַל־כָּל־הָאָרֶץ, הַיּוֹשֵׁב עַל־כִּסֵּא רַחֲמִים,
שֶׁיִּתְגּוֹלֲלוּ רַחֲמֶיךָ עָלֵינוּ, וְתִתְנַהֵג בְּחַסְדְּךָ עִמָּנוּ,
וְאַל־תָּבוֹא בְּמִשְׁפָּט עִמָּנוּ, כִּי לֹא יִצְדַּק לְפָנֶיךָ כָּל־
חָי. עֲמוֹד מִכִּסֵּא דִינֶךָ, וְשֵׁב עַל־כִּסֵּא רַחֲמֶיךָ,
וְרַחֵם עַל־עַמֶּךָ, הַקּוֹרְאִים לִשְׁמֶךָ, וְזָכְרֵנוּ בְּזִכְרוֹן
טוֹב לְפָנֶיךָ, וַעֲשֵׂה לְמַעַנְךָ וּלְמַעַן שׁוֹכְנֵי עָפָר
הַקְּדוֹשִׁים אֲשֶׁר בָּאָרֶץ הֵמָּה, כִּי לְךָ עֵינֵינוּ
מְיַחֲלוֹת וְלִתְשׁוּעָתְךָ מְקַוּוֹת, צַדְּקֵנוּ בְּדִינֶךָ, וְנִזָּכֵר

(נערב ראש השנה.)   (נערב יום כפור.)

וְנִכָּתֵב לְפָנֶיךָ בְּסֵפֶר | וְנֵחָתֵם לְפָנֶיךָ בְּסֵפֶר
הַחַיִּים לְטוֹבָה וְלִבְרָכָה | הַחַיִּים בְּזֶה יוֹם
בְּזֶה רֹאשׁ הַשָּׁנָה | צוֹם הַכִּפֻּרִים הַבָּא

Grant to remove from us, and from all the people of the house of Israel, trouble, sorrow, affliction and evil mishaps. Amen.

PRAYER ON VISITING THE BURIAL GROUND ON THE DAY BEFORE NEW YEAR (ערב ראש השנה) AND ON THE DAY BEFORE YOM KIPPUR.

May it be acceptable in Thy presence, Thou, eternal God of mercy and forgiveness, who sittest on the throne of mercy, to incline Thy tender compassion towards us, and to look down from Thy celestial seat on Thy [servant] [handmaid], who with a trembling heart and a contrite spirit ventures to approach this awful and sacred spot of the pious ones, who repose here in peace, to invoke Thy paternal forgiveness for the sins, iniquities and transgressions which I have committed. Enter not into rigorous judgment with us; for no one can be justified before Thee. Alas, I feel my unworthiness, I am conscious of my transgressions; yet do it for Thy sake and for the sake of the merit of the holy ones, who slumber in the dust; for, unto Thee and for Thy salvation are our eyes continually directed, that Thou mayest justify us in Thy judgment.

[On the Day before the New Year.]

Grant that we may on the ensuing morning of the New Year, that

[On the day before the Day of Atonement.]

Grant that we may on the ensuing morning, the day of fasting and atone-

הַבָּא עָלֵינוּ לְטוֹבָה ׀ עָלֵינוּ לְטוֹבָה וְלִבְרָכָה
וְלִמְחִילָה וְלִסְלִיחָה עַל־כָּל־חַטֹּאתֵינוּ שֶׁחָטָאנוּ
וְשֶׁעָוִינוּ וְשֶׁפָּשַׁעְנוּ לְפָנֶיךָ. וְתִגְזֹר עָלֵינוּ שָׁנָה טוֹבָה
לְחַיִּים טוֹבִים וּלְשָׁלוֹם, שְׁנַת אֱמֶת, שְׁנַת בְּרָכָה,
שְׁנַת גְּאֻלָּה, שְׁנַת דִּיצָה, שְׁנַת הוֹד, שְׁנַת וָעַד טוֹב,
שְׁנַת זִכָּרוֹן, שְׁנַת חֶדְוָה, שְׁנַת טוֹבָה, שְׁנַת יְשׁוּעָה,
שְׁנַת כַּלְכָּלָה, שְׁנַת לִמּוּד, שְׁנַת מְנוּחָה, שְׁנַת
נֶחָמָה, שְׁנַת סַיַּעְתָּא, שְׁנַת עֶזְרָה, שְׁנַת פְּדוּת,
שְׁנַת צְדָקָה, שְׁנַת קְדֻשָּׁה, שְׁנַת רָצוֹן, שְׁנַת
שָׁלוֹם, שְׁנַת תְּשׁוּעָתֵנוּ. וְתִתֵּן בְּרָכָה בְּמַעֲשֵׂה יָדֵינוּ
וּתְמַלֵּא כָּל־בַּקָּשׁוֹתֵינוּ וּצְרָכֵינוּ. וְתִזְקוֹף לְמַעְלָה
קַרְנֵנוּ, וְתֹאמַר דַּי לְצָרוֹתֵינוּ וְקֵץ וְסוֹף לְגָלוּתֵנוּ.
וּתְמַהֵר לְגָאֳלֵנוּ. כַּפֵּר לְעַמְּךָ יִשְׂרָאֵל הַחַיִּים
עוֹדֶנָּה, וְלַאֲשֶׁר פָּדִיתָ יְיָ וְיִצְאָה נַפְשָׁם מִנֶּדְנָה:

(בטיב יום כפור מוסיף וּבְיוֹם הַכִּפּוּרִים הַזֶּה תְּכַפֵּר
עָלֵינוּ. לְטַהֵר אוֹתָנוּ מִכָּל־חַטֹּאתֵינוּ. וְלִפְנֵי יְיָ
יִטְהָר כָּל־אָדָם מֵחוֹבוֹ בְּיוֹם הַדִּין הַגָּדוֹל) : זְכוֹר יְיָ
לִבְנֵי אָדָם הַקְּדוֹשִׁים אֲשֶׁר בָּאָרֶץ הֵמָּה הָאֵתָנִים
מוֹסְדֵי תֵבֵל, בִּזְכוּתָם וּבִזְכוּת כָּל־יִשְׁנֵי עָפָר תַּשְׁבִּית
מִמֶּנּוּ וּמִכָּל־עַמְּךָ בֵּית יִשְׂרָאֵל כָּל־צָרָה וְיָגוֹן וְאַף
וְחָרוֹן, וּתְמַלֵּא בַקָּשָׁתֵנוּ וְתִשְׁלַח לָנוּ מְשִׁיחֵנוּ,
וְתִבְנֶה לָנוּ בֵּית קָדְשֵׁנוּ, וְתַחֲזִיר שְׁכִינָתְךָ לְאַרְצֵנוּ,
וְתֵטִיב לָנוּ אַחֲרִיתֵנוּ, וְהַט חַסְדְּךָ עָלֵינוּ, כִּי אַתָּה

draws   near   to   us,   be | ment, that draws towards
remembered   and   in- | us, be remembered and
scribed   scaled
in the book of a happy life and of blessing, to pardon
and forgiveness for all our sins and transgressions.
Father of mercy! Grant us a happy and blessed
year, a year of felicity, of peace, of truth, of redemption, of gladness, of honor, of good assembly, of sub-
sistence, of enlightenment, of ease, of consolation, of
Divine assistance, of piety, of sanctity, of peace and
of salvation. Deign to send Thy blessings on our
undertakings, grant our requests, and fulfil our desires; exalt our horn on high, terminate our sufferings,
collect our dispersed, and hasten to redeem us.
Pardon the sins of Thy people of Israel, who are
yet alive, and of those whose souls have quitted their
earthly coils. *[Pardon and cleanse us on the approaching sacred Day of Atonement from our sins,
so that all may be free from guilt on the great and
awful day of judgment, as indicated in the Day of
Atonement.

May the godly and meritorious deeds of those
pious ones who repose here, and of those who sleep
in Hebron, be extended to us, to remove from me
and from all Thy people of the house of Israel all
wrath and anger, so that I may not quit fruitlessly
this awful place. Send us Thine anointed one, re-
build for us Thy sacred house, restore Thy Divine
glory to our glorious land, and deal with us bountifully in our latter end. May Thy paternal mercy
prevail over us; for Thou art our God. Hear us, O

*On the day before יוֹם הַכִּפּוּר add.

אֱלֹהֵינוּ. שְׁמַע יְיָ אֱלֹהֵינוּ, וּתְקַבֵּל בְּרַחֲמִים וּבְרָצוֹן
אֵת תְּפִלָּתֵנוּ:

SHORT PRAYER ADAPTED FOR VISITING
THE GRAVE OF EITHER FATHER, MOTH-
ER, SON, DAUGHTER, BROTHER OR SIS-
TER, RELATIVES AND FRIENDS.

יִזְכֹּר אֱלֹהִים אֶת־נִשְׁמָתְךָ לְטוֹבָה (בשנה ראשונה

למיתתו יוסיף וְיִשְׁמָרְךָ מֵחִבּוּט הַקֶּבֶר מֵרִמָּה וְתוֹלֵעָה)

וְתִישַׁן שְׁנַת עֲרֵבָה . וְתָנוּחַ בְּקִבְרְךָ בִּמְנוּחָה
נְכוֹנָה . וּזְכוּתְךָ תָּגֵן עָלַי כְּעֵת צָרָתִי . וְנִשְׁמָתְךָ
תְּהִי צְרוּרָה בִּצְרוֹר הַחַיִּים עִם־שְׁאָר צַדִּיקִים
וְצִדְקָנִיּוֹת שֶׁבְּגַן עֵדֶן, אָמֵן:

PRAYER ON QUITTING THE BURIAL
GROUND.

שָׁלוֹם עֲלֵיכֶן הַנְּשָׁמוֹת הַטְּהוֹרוֹת, נֶאֱצָלוֹת מִזִּיו
יוֹצֵר הַמְּאוֹרוֹת: הִנְנִי הוֹלֵךְ לְדַרְכִּי, וְנַפְשִׁי אֶת־יְיָ
בָּרֲכִי, וּלְאֵל חַי תְּפִלָּתִי, יִשְׁמָר־בִּי רוּחִי וְנִשְׁמָתִי,
יִשְׁמַע עֲתִירַת דּוֹרְשָׁיו, יַרְבֶּה כְּבוֹד שְׁלֵמָיו, יוֹסִיף
חֵן וָחֶסֶד לַעֲנָוָיו הַקְּדוֹשִׁים עֹשֵׂי מִצְוֹתָיו: וּכְכֵן נוּחוּ,

Eternal, and accept our prayers with mercy and favor! Amen.

___

SHORT PRAYER ADAPTED FOR VISITING THE GRAVE OF EITHER FATHER, MOTH- ER, SON, DAUGHTER, BROTHER OR SIS- TER, RELATIVES AND FRIENDS.

May God remember thy soul for good. *[May He preserve thee from the terror of the grave.]

May He grant unto thee a sweet slumber, and mayest thou rest in the grave in perfect ease. May the merit of thy pious deeds be extended to us in the time of trouble, and thy soul be treasured up in the treasure of life, in association with all the pious ones in Israel.

___

PRAYER ON QUITTING THE BURIAL GROUND.

Peace be unto you, ye pure beatified souls, ema- nations from the effulgence of Him who created the luminaries. Behold, I go my way, and my soul blesses the Eternal, the God of life, to whom I direct my prayer. O may He deign to guard within me my soul and spirit; may He hear the prayers of those who seek Him, increase the honor of His perfect ones, and heap grace and mercy on His pious and meek in the land, who perform His command- ments: so that they may see their descendants grow strong in health, and in the fear of God, and cause them to behold the solemn assembly in the sacred temple.

___
* At the grave of those departed within a year add.

יְשָׁרִים נוֹחוּ, עַד יֵעָרֶה עָלֵיכֶם רוּחַ מִמָּרוֹם, וִיאֹמֶר
שׁוֹכֵן מָרוֹם אֲדוֹן הַחַיִּים, עִמְדוּ יְשָׁרִים וְשׁוּבוּ
לְחַיִּים, וְאָו תָּקִיצוּ וּתְרַנֵּנוּ וְתָקוּמוּ וְתִחְיוּ: וַאֲנַחְנוּ
נִכְנֵס לְחַיִּים טוֹבִים וּלְשָׁלוֹם, עַד אֲשֶׁר יְקָרֵב הֲלוֹם
צִיר נֶאֱמָן מְשִׁיחַ אֱלֹהֵי יַעֲקֹב, וְהֵשִׁיב לֵב אָבוֹת
עַל־בָּנִים וְלֵב בָּנִים עַל־אֲבוֹתָם, וְצֶדֶק יְהַלֵּךְ לְפָנֵינוּ,
וּנְהַלֵּל וּנְשַׁבֵּחַ לֵאלֹהֵינוּ עָשָׂה גְדֹלוֹת עַד־אֵין חֵקֶר
וְנִפְלָאוֹת עַד־אֵין מִסְפָּר, הוּא הָאֵל הַגָּדוֹל וְהַגִּבּוֹר,
מַתִּיר אֲסוּרִים בִּדְבָרוֹ, מְחַיֵּה מֵתִים בְּמַאֲמָרוֹ
בָּרוּךְ הוּא מְחַיֵּה הַמֵּתִים:

PRAYER FOR DAILY BREAD.

To be recited on the graveyard.

יְהִי רָצוֹן לְפָנֶיךָ יְיָ אֱלֹהֵינוּ וֵאלֹהֵי אֲבוֹתֵינוּ שֶׁיִּהְיוּ
מְזוֹנוֹתַי וּמְזוֹנוֹת בְּנֵי בֵיתִי עִם־מְזוֹנוֹת כָּל־עַמְּךָ בֵּית
יִשְׂרָאֵל מְכֻתָּרִים וּמְאֻמָּתִים וּמְצֻדָּקִים בְּיָדֶךָ, וְאַל־
תַּצְרִיכֵנִי לִידֵי מַתְּנַת בָּשָׂר וָדָם וְלֹא לִידֵי הַלְוָאָתָם
כִּי אִם לְיָדְךָ הַמְּלֵאָה הַפְּתוּחָה וְהָרְחָבָה, וּתְהִי
מְלַאכְתִּי וְכָל־עֵסְקִי לִבְרָכָה וְלֹא לַעֲנִיּוּת, לְחַיִּים
וְלֹא לְמָוֶת, וּתְזַכֵּנִי שֶׁלֹּא יִתְחַלֵּל שֵׁם שָׁמַיִם עַל־יָדִי,
וְאֶהְיֶה מִן־הַמּוֹעִילִים וּמַשְׁפִּיעִים טוֹב לְכָל־אָדָם
תָּמִיד, וּתְמַלֵּא יָדַי מִבִּרְכוֹתֶיךָ וְשַׂבְּעֵנִי מִטּוּבֶךָ, כִּי

Thus rest, rest in peace, ye upright slumberers! Repose until the King of life, the Lord of heaven and earth, will exclaim: "Rise, ye upright ones! Rise to everlasting life!"

Source of life! Grant that we may enter into a life of happiness and peace, until the faithful messenger will draw near, and the anointed of the God of Jacob, and affectionately restore the hearts of parents to children, and the hearts of children to parents, and when righteousness will precede us. We will then praise and adore our God with all praises and glorifications; for He is great, mighty and tremendous. He revives the dead by His mere word, who does great and unsearchable deeds, marvellous things without number. Blessed be He who reviveth the dead.

PRAYER FOR DAILY BREAD.

To be recited on the graveyard.

May it be Thy will, O Lord, our God, and God of our fathers, that my daily sustenance, and that of all thy people Israel, proceed from Thine hand, so that it always should be plentiful and honorable. Let me never depend upon the gifts or loans of man: but let me ever depend on Thy bountiful hand. May all my labor be fruitful, and may it never be barren. May my work lead to life, not to death. May Thy sacred name never become desecrated through me; and may I be one of those that promote good among mankind. Fill my hands with Thy blessings, and my heart with Thy goodness.

אַתָּה יְיָ בֵּרַכְתָּ וּמְבָרֵךְ לְעוֹלָם, עֵינֵי כֹל אֵלֶיךָ
יְשַׂבֵּרוּ וְאַתָּה נוֹתֵן־לָהֶם אֶת־אָכְלָם בְּעִתּוֹ. פּוֹתֵחַ
אֶת־יָדֶךָ וּמַשְׂבִּיעַ לְכָל־חַי רָצוֹן. עָלֶיךָ יְיָ אַשְׁלִיךְ
יְהָבִי וְאַתָּה תְכַלְכְּלֵנִי:

וְאַתָּן נִשְׁמוֹת הַקְּדוֹשִׁים וְהַטְּהוֹרִים הַעֲטֵרְנָה
אֵלַּיְיָ בַּעֲדִי, שִׁירִים קַרְנִי וַיַגְבִּיהַ מַזָּלִי, לְמַעַן אוּכַל
לַעֲבֹדוֹ בְּלֵבָב שָׁלֵם כָּל־יְמֵי חַיָּי. וּבְשֵׁם טוֹב וּבְשָׁעָה
טוֹבָה אֶפָּטֵר מִן־הָעוֹלָם הַזֶּה, וִיהִי חֶלְקִי עִמָּכֶן
בְּגַן עֵדֶן, אָמֵן:

PRAYER FOR FORGIVENESS OF SIN COM-
MITTED AGAINST DEPARTED ONES.

שָׁלוֹם עָלֶיךָ אַתָּה רוּחַ הַקָּדוֹשׁ וְהַטָּהוֹר. וְשָׁלוֹם
לְנַפְשֶׁךָ וּלְנִשְׁמָתְךָ בַּשְּׁחָקִים בָּהִיר. מְנוּחָתְךָ תִּהְיֶה
שְׁלֵמָה. לְמַעְלָה מִמַּלְאֲכֵי רוּמָה. וְעַצְמוֹתֶיךָ יָנוּחוּ
בְּקֶבֶר בְּשָׁלוֹם עַל־מִשְׁכָּבָן: וַאֲנִי עָנִי וְכוֹאֵב. מְחוֹלָל
מִפְּשָׁעִים וַחֲטָאִים שׁוֹאֵב. בָּאתִי הֵנָּה לִמְקוֹם
קְבוּרָתְךָ וּלְבֵית מִשְׁכָּבְךָ. לְהִתְחַנֵּן לְךָ וּלְפַיְּסָךְ
עַל אֲשֶׁר פָּעַלְתִּי וְדִבַּרְתִּי וְעָלוּ עַל־לִבִּי דְבָרִים
שֶׁהֵם נֶגֶד כְּבוֹדְךָ וְזִיוְךָ וַהֲדָרְךָ וְהוֹדֶךָ, וְהִנְנִי מוֹדֶה
וְעוֹזֵב וְאוֹמֵר נַעֲנֵיתִי לְךָ (פלוני) כִּי חָטָאתִי לַיְיָ
אֱלֹהֵי יִשְׂרָאֵל וְלָךְ. וְכָל־מַה שֶׁהִרְהַרְתִּי וְדִבַּרְתִּי

Thou alone blessest all. The eyes of all are directed to Thee; and Thou givest to all their food in due time. Thou openest Thy hand and satisfiest all living in mercy. I cast my burden upon Thee and Thou wilt sustain me.

And ye pure souls! pray for me, that my lot be blessed: so that I may serve God with a perfect heart all my lifetime; and that I may go hence into life immortal, when my day will come, and leave behind me a good name; and then dwell in your midst in the heavenly Eden above. Amen.

PRAYER FOR FORGIVENESS OF SIN COMMITTED AGAINST DEPARTED ONES.

To be recited on the grave.

Peace be with thee, hallowed and purified spirit, now resting in the bright realms on high! Perfect peace with thee, who dwellest now with the angels above, whilst thy mortal remains repose in the quiet grave. But, alas! I am pained and oppressed by sin and iniquity; and hither I came now to this, thy dark grave, to ask forgiveness from thy spirit for all the wrong I have done or meditated to do to thee when living with us on earth. Behold, I confess, I acted wrong against thee (*N. N.*,) I have sinned against the law of God in striving to harm thy name, or in neglecting to fulfil my obligations toward thee.

וְעָשִׂיתִי וּפָעַלְתִּי נֶגְדֶּךָ, אוֹ כָּל־מָה אֲשֶׁר הִתְרַשַּׁלְתִּי
מֵעֲשׂוֹת לִכְבוֹדֶךָ, הַכֹּל הָיָה אֶצְלִי בִּשְׁגָגָה יוֹצֵאת
מִדַּעַת מְטָעָה, וְכָל־אֲשֶׁר עָשִׂיתִי שֶׁלֹּא כַהֹגֶן הִנְנִי
מִתְחָרֵט עָלָיו בַּחֲרָטָה גְמוּרָה . וַאֲבַקֶּשְׁךָ שֶׁיִּכְמְרוּ
נָא רַחֲמֶיךָ עָלַי וְתַעֲמוֹד בִּתְפִלָּה וּבְבַקָּשָׁה לִפְנֵי
מֶלֶךְ מַלְכֵי הַמְּלָכִים הַקָּדוֹשׁ בָּרוּךְ הוּא, שֶׁיִּמְחַל
לִי בְּרֹב רַחֲמָיו וַחֲסָדָיו עַל־כָּל־מָה שֶׁחָטָאתִי
וְעָוִיתִי וּפָשַׁעְתִּי הֵן נֶגְדּוֹ וְהֵן נֶגֶד בְּרִיּוֹתָיו, וְיַעֲזָר־לִי
בְּרֹב רַחֲמָיו וַחֲסָדָיו לִשְׁמוֹר מִצְוֹתָיו . וְאַל־יַטְרִידֵנִי
מַטְרֵד וּמַשְׂטִין . וְעַל־מֵי מְנוּחוֹת יְנַהֲלֵנִי . וְיַאֲרִיךְ
יָמַי וּשְׁנוֹתַי בַּנְּעִימִים . וְאַךְ טוֹב וָחֶסֶד יִרְדְּפוּנִי
כָּל־יְמֵי חַיַּי וְשַׁבְתִּי בְּבֵית יְיָ לְאֹרֶךְ יָמִים. אָמֵן סֶלָה:

With a contrite heart I repent all I have done against thee, all I have thought against thee. O! that thy pity may be moved and thy prayers may be active for me, that the Lord God, blessed be His name, may pardon all my sins: and all my transgressions against His law and against His creatures may be blotted out; and that His help may be extended to me, that I may cling to His law without stint or hindrance. And may the Lord lead me henceforth on the still waters of peace, and happiness and grace may be my portion all the days of my life, so that I may always dwell in the House of God. Amen.

ADDITIONAL PRAYERS.

---o---

PRAYERS FOR THE SICK.

PRAYER FOR A SICK HUSBAND.

From the depth of my heart I call upon Thee, O my Lord. Awful is the darkness that surrounds me on account of the sickness of my beloved husband. With a contrite, anxious and lacerated heart I implore Thee, that Thou mayest preserve unto me, yet for many, many years, the precious treasure which Thou, in Thy grace, didst vouchsafe unto me.

Refreshed by no slumber nor rest, the nights pass away before me; bitter woe is my severe companion, for the happiness of my family lies prostrate, the crown of my house is surrounded by dark clouds. O Lord! hearken unto my prayer,—remove this heavy weight from my heart! Do not deprive me of the dearest and highest of all treasures, do not tear the heart from the heart!

But the hope written within my heart, by the belief of my fathers, speaks unto me with consoling words: "Confide,—and endure, whatever the Lord may have ordained for thee!" Yes, I wait upon Thy paternal grace, I trust in Thy mercy, as the

sacred bard teaches me : "He that trusteth in the Lord, mercy shall compass him about." Return, O God! unto my beloved husband, his former strength and vigor, return him unto his sacred duties, and let him work, yet for many years, for the welfare of our family! Oh! may this be Thy holy will. Amen.

PRAYER FOR SICK PARENTS.

More in tears than in words is my prayer poured forth this day, before Thee, All-merciful Father! in tears burning and abundant, produced by woe and anxiety! For what is more saddening for the heart of a child than to know that a dear parent is pros-trated upon the couch of sufferings and sickness? And however much I trust and hope in Thy mercy, yet with trembling and alarm I bow before Thee, to implore of Thee the life, the health of my beloved *(father—mother)*. Thou hast proclaimed the word : *"Ye shall seek my face!"* I seek Thy face with a longing heart. Oh! do not hide it from me. Hearken unto my fervent prayer,—let not my tears flow in vain before Thee, have mercy upon my dear *(father —mother)*, quicken *(him—her)* with the soft dew of Thy grace, mercifully pour Thy healing balm upon *(his—her)* wounds, and let the rays of Thy goodness and compassion descend upon *(him—her)*, that *(he —she)* may be uplifted by their warmth and restored to strength and vigor. Forgive *(him—her)*, O All-

good Father! whenever and wherever (*he—she*) may have erred, and remember all the good and charitable deeds which (*he—she*) may have performed,—Oh! let these deeds now intercede for (*him—her*) before Thy throne of justice and mercy.

May my fervent prayer come before Thee, that the hour of deliverance and salvation may soon arrive, and our tears of woe be turned into tears of joy and gratitude. Amen. _____

PRAYER FOR A SICK CHILD.

O All-merciful Father! from the depth of my aggrieved heart I implore Thee: spare my child, do not take away this treasure that Thou gavest unto me from Thine boundless grace and goodness. I know this treasure is *Thine,* as all other boons which I call mine; Thou disposest of them according to Thy holy will. O! may it be Thy holy will to preserve for me this precious jewel! Once Thou spokest unto Thy suffering Congregation: "*Call unto me in need, and I shall hear thee!*" And through the inspired Isaiah Thou gavest the consoling assurance unto Thy people Israel: "*I will pour my spirit upon thy children, and my blessing upon thine offspring!*" Oh! extend this paternal promise also upon my child, grant him (*her*) health and long life.

And unto me grant strength in all the cares and trials of life, fortify my courage in the fulfillment of my duties and in the endurance of all the heavy bur-

dens that Thy paternal hands may impose upon me. In Thee, O God! I trust, for Thou art nigh unto all who call upon Thee. Amen.

PRAYER IN HEAVY SICKNESS.

O Lord! answer and compassionate me, for I am full of distress, and humbled in mine afflictions. I am bowed down with weakness as a child, and without Thine aid, how shall I bear my troubles? Oh, that my deeds had been worthy of Thine approbation, then had my soul been satisfied and my heart rejoiced. Yet, do Thou, O God! regard my contrition, hear my prayer, and lend Thy mercy even as a staff for my support. O Lord! pains and evils are inherited with the nature of man, yet my soul shall not be shaken by their approach. For, on whom shall I call for help but on Thee? And where shall I rest my hope but in Thy mercies? *"Though my flesh and my heart fail, God is my consolation, my portion for ever ; for, lo, they that are far from Thee shall perish, they that go after the favor of others shall be destroyed."* Ah! were my days of sorrow lengthened to the number of mine offences, yet, O Lord! I would still bless Thy name, and Thy dispensations, for Thou art my consolation, the resting place of my soul. Then, wherefore should I complain? I will resign myself to Thy will, for Thou, O Lord! art the Author of my being, and wilt not destroy the work

which Thou hast made.   Then shall I profit from
my woes, and all times rest in Thy hands; for Thou,
O my God! art my Savior and my living Redeemer.
Amen.

PRAYERS FOR THE DEAD.

REFLECTIONS.

How dare we, inhabiting this frail clay, raise our
eyes in pride.   Should we not rather remember that
our body, like that of the crawling worm, will soon
be mingled with the dust?

Man is vainly proud of his reason and intellect;
yet these treasures cannot save him from the decrees of divine justice, if he wickedly makes a wrong
use of these possessions.

Let us reflect then, whence do we come, and
whither are we going.   Human life is limited like
that of the plant; a day may destroy what the pre-
ceding one has produced.   Is it not better to die in
righteousness, than to fall a prey to temptation and
sin in the pursuit of the perishable wealth and
fleeting power of this world?

Frail from our birth, we consume our energies in
toil after riches; the body resists the call of religion
so long as it remains animated by the soul; but when

this departs, what is left? Naught but clay and ashes. Of what avail therefore are dignity and riches? will they not be left to strangers? do we not return naked as we came? why, then, should we listen to the voice of passion? why are we intoxicated with success, when such is sure to be our end?

Let us cast aside all iniquity, amend our conduct, and return to our Father, the King of kings; for repentance and prayer will obtain His mercy. Let us examine our ways, and think of our end, for we know not when the day of death will come. Let us lift up our hearts to God; for we have been led away by worldly illusions, and have been wandering astray, like sheep without a shepherd.

May the death of him for whom we now mourn, cause us to repent while there is yet time; for we know not when we may be summoned before the tribunal of the MOST HIGH.

Grant, O Lord! that this warning may not be lost to us; but do Thou assist us to make a proper use of our days on earth, so that we may employ them righteously, and secure thus our salvation. Call us not unprepared, we beseech Thee, into Thy presence, until we shall have been able to efface our sins by pious acts and righteous deeds. Amen.

MEDITATIONS AND PRAYERS ON VISITING THE GRAVES OF THOSE WE LOVED.

My soul is filled with sadness on entering this mournful abode of the dead. Here are ended all human projects and desires, passions and endeavors; pride and lowliness, wealth and poverty, love and hate, all sleep here alike in peace.

How terrible would be our anguish and despair, if faith did not reveal to us the immortal destiny of the soul! Were we not to acknowledge a future responsibility, there would be no such impulse as duty; the loftiest sentiments, therefore, the holiest affections, would lose their incentive, and remain uncultivated as useless emotions.

But *all* ends not here. Death is not annihilation; it is but the entrance to a better existence, and leads to eternal life; for in death the soul casts off its material garment to enter the abode of immortality.

Those loved ones, whose ashes repose beneath this sod, are not eternally lost to us; they live in the presence of our Creator, and their graves serve as a memorial to those who loved them in life, and hope to be united to them in eternity. O ye whom I have loved so tenderly! although you repose now on your last bed of rest, you will live forever in my heart, I pray for you on earth; as I feel that you watch over me in the abode of the blest, where I hope, one day, our souls will be united in glory.

These consoling thoughts dispel the gloom of this mournful spot, where I, in my turn, must one day seek my rest. The grave is the gate which opens for us a new state of existence, where our good works are our only true possessions; these are never lost, and will obtain for us grace in the sight of Him who is our impartial Judge. O God! regard with pity those who sleep here in their last resting place; may their good deeds, their earthly sufferings, and the pangs of death, be regarded by Thee as a ransom for their souls; and may it please Thee to appoint their portion in eternal bliss.

Guide me, O Heavenly Father! during my earthly pilgrimage; so that when it shall please Thee to call me hence, my soul may appear worthy of Thy salvation. Amen.

ON THE ANNIVERSARY OF A PARENT'S DEATH. *(JAHRZEIT.)*

This day recalls to my mind the solemn and sorrowful day on which the soul of my beloved (*father* —*mother*) departed from its earthly tenement, on which the eye broke that once so lovingly and tenderly rested upon me, on which the hand was palsied in death that once so faithfully guided and supported me—a day of painful recollection, of ever renewed mourning! The ever honored picture of my dear parent appears before my soul, the breath of the

sainted spirit is fanning upon me. How could the memory of the glorified being ever vanish from my heart and soul? As long as I shall walk upon this earth, this sacred memory shall be faithfully enshrined within the inmost recesses of my soul, until I also shall conclude my earthly career and meet again the loving and loved being whose loss I deeply mourn.

Father of life! I pray Thee to vouchsafe rest unto the soul of my sainted (*father—mother*). May (*his—her*) spirit have found peace upon the heights of eternal light,—pure, undimmed peace unto all eternity! May (*his—her*) soul be bound in the eternal bond of life. May it tarry before Thee in purity and salvation! And for me, (*his—her*) earthly child, who still walks in the shadows of this world, subject to changing fortune, to error and sin, may that sainted soul intercede before Thy throne, that I may be protected upon all my ways and deserve Thy grace. O Lord! Thou givest, Thou takest away, Thy name be praised for ever and ever. Amen.

AT A FATHER'S GRAVE.

All-merciful God! In this silent field, where the earthly remains of my departed father rest, I will dedicate my filial tears and emotions unto his memory. Now, that I have lost him, the dear one, for this earthly life, I fully know what treasure of love I

once possessed in him. He, the faithful guide of my youth, my monitor and counsellor, did attend, with wise circumspection to the ennoblement of my spirit and the strengthening of my body; he illumined my mind and filled my heart with love; he submitted joyfully to all *the struggles of life*, in order to procure to his child *the joys of life*. O my dear father—while I remember thee, my tears are streaming forth, and my heart is overflowing with love and grief. But what can my love profit thee now? It can no longer cause thee *earthly joy and earthly happiness*, who are far removed from all *earthly wishes, earthly wants, and earthly cares!*

But doing good, practising charity, ennobling the heart—these are *heavenly joys* which a child may prepare for his glorified and sainted father. And these joys I will prepare for thee, by performing good actions in thy name and in thy spirit;—these shall be the sacrifices to be offered up by me upon the altar of my filial love,—may God record them in His book of eternal life, unto thy beatitude and salvation in thy heavenly habitation!

O God of heaven and earth! as my sainted father has left behind, *in paternal love*, his blessings, thus do I, in return, *from filial love*, bless his memory before Thee, and pray unto Thee for the salvation of his soul. Oh! mayest Thou also remember him in love and mercy, mayest Thou remember every noble deed, every good action which he performed on this

earth, and graciously forgive whatever sin and transgression he may have committed from human weakness. And may all his sufferings, troubles, tribulations and hardships which he had to endure during his earthly sojourn, be his atonement and propitiation before Thee, that he may be a partaker of eternal peace, beatitude and salvation in Thy divine presence. Amen.

____

AT A FATHER'S GRAVE.

My father, my kindest friend, my dearest benefactor, whom God had appointed to love and protect me, reposes in this silent grave. I shall never hear again his dear voice; death has stilled his loving heart; his friendship and kindness can no longer comfort, neither can his counsels and example guide me. Alas! I cannot now make a return for his devotion or loving kindness, nor have the happiness of surrounding his old age with marks of respect and solicitude; but I will strive to show my respect for his memory by deeds of righteousness and obedience to his expressed wishes while he was yet on earth, and this endeavor will surely bring me consolation. Assist me in this, O God! with Thy counsel, inspire me with wisdom and intelligence, and enlighten me that I may follow the right path. Cause my works on earth to reflect honor on my father's memory, and do Thou, Lord! accept them as an expiatory sacrifice for any sins he has committed.

I beseech Thee! receive my father's soul among Thy faithful servants; and when my hour shall come, grant that my spirit may likewise be united with these in a life which is unending.

Rest in peace, O my father! and may thy spirit enjoy, in eternity, the contemplation of the living God. Amen.

AT A MOTHER'S GRAVE.

My dear, beloved mother, who sleepest beneath this sod, for ever laid at rest in the lap of earth—thy child draws nigh to thee with the tear of mourning in her eyes, burning even as on the day when they brought thee hither. Thy spirit sojourns upon the heights of eternal light, but couldst thou ever forget thy child, still walking in the shadows of earth? No! a mother's love is everlasting, eternal, even as her soul is eternal, even as God is eternal who implanted that love in her heart! In pain thou gavest me life, and yet thou didst greet me with a gladsome smile when I lay in thy arms;—thus thou didst ever endure the sufferings of life and accept them with a mother's smile.—What trouble is there, that thou wouldst shun, what care that thou wouldst not endure for me? As thou wouldst watch at my bed of sickness, —as thou wouldst sacrifice all for me,—as thy first and thy last glance at me was full of self-sacrificing love,—as thy heart excused even my failings, and

thy tear shed at my error was at the same time a
tear of forgiveness—O sacred spirit of my mother!
behold the tears flowing forth from the eye of thy
child in the memory of thee,—they are all that I
can yet offer unto thee, accept them as a sacrifice
of thanks and love!—

Didst not thou teach my lips the first word of
prayer and direct the child's emotions up to God?
Didst not thou implant pious thoughts in the heart
of thy child? Didst not thou guide my first steps in
life, and watch over me day and night? Yea, unto
thee I am indebted for the germs of all that is good,
for the indestructible seeds of piety, religion and
virtue! Yea, here I confess it and spread my confes-
sion as a lucid shroud upon thy grave.

How couldst thou be separated from me, though
removed from this earth? I feel thy presence by
the warm stream of feelings flowing through my soul
at this moment. Yea, thou dost still bear with me
all my grief, rejoicest in my joys, mournest over my
aberrations—but thou dwellest in the light of knowledge and truth, and knowest the end, and the eva-
nescence of all that is earthly, and art conscious of
the mercy of God, and, therefore, at ease on account
of all my destinies, and invisibly inspirest me with
comfort and courage. Thus then I will again, near
this thy sleeping-place, resolve firmly and solemnly,
to live in thy spirit, to walk in the path of duty and
virtue, piety and religion, worthy of thee, unto thy

honor and satisfaction. Whatever dispensation may come upon me, I will endure it in memory of thee, as though thou still didst walk before me, admonish and warn me,—as though thine eye did still see all my actions, until my hour of departure also shall come, and my spirit ascend to yonder heights, there to be received by thee!

Eternal Father in heaven! preserve peace on this consecrated grave which I irrigate with my tears, that the honored remains of my beloved mother may rest therein undisturbed! And unto her glorified soul mayest Thou vouchsafe an eternal abode of bliss, in which the noble, pure spirit may behold Thy countenance in everlasting joy. Amen.

AT A MOTHER'S GRAVE.

"The Lord gave, the Lord hath taken away, blessed be the name of the Lord." (Job i, 21.) It has been Thy will, O God! to take my beloved mother from me. This earth covers the precious remains of her who was devoted during her earthly existence to the well-being of her children. She rejoiced with us in our joy, and sorrowed with us in our grief; she lived only to promote our happiness. Her body lies here, beneath this cold earth, and I only shed fruitless tears on her silent tomb.

I come hither, O mother! to honor thy revered memory, and to commune, in thought, with thy spirit.

My heart seems to feel that thy tender love still watches over me; thy dear voice still appears to bid me follow the duties of religion towards God and mankind. O may I in performing good deeds on this earth, and following thy bright example, prove my veneration for thy memory, and obtain forgiveness for the pains and tears I have cost thee.

O deeply loved mother! may thy pure soul, now released from its earthly bonds, experience heavenly joy; and look on me with love and pity.

Merciful Father! hearken to the prayers of a child, who implores Thy favor for his (*her*) mother. Have compassion, judge her leniently, and receive her soul in mercy into the home of the blessed, so that she may rejoice eternally in Thy goodness. Amen.

AT A HUSBAND'S GRAVE.

Hither, unto the silent dwelling-place of death, my heart, sad and dreary even as this place, feels attracted. Surrounded by the night of the grave my beloved husband rests here, and my burning tears may flow upon his tomb, my lamentation be poured forth in undisturbed currents. Far from the tumult of life, no stranger's eye, no unsympathetic word desecrates my grief; Thou alone, O my God, art witness to the pain that has taken root in the depth of my soul, causing life with all its beauties to appear dark to me, and all its joys to seem covered as with a veil of mourning.

Mayest Thou, O Father of all, not be angry with me, that I lament thus bitterly, that my soul mourns so deeply over that which Thou hast ordained. My God! I do not take upon myself to murmur against Thy dispensations and to censure Thy ways. Thou art the God of love and wisdom; what mortal could perceive and understand Thee? Who could presume to judge Thy ways and ask Thee: "What doest Thou?" Whatever Thou doest is well done,—therefore do I in the dust adore Thee and in humility pay homage to Thine inscrutable counsel. But can I command my heart not to feel my misfortune? Can I say to my grief: "Flee from me!" to my mourning soul: "Be cheerful!"?

And why should my soul not mourn, now that its other half has been separated from it; why should mine eyes not be filled with tears, now that the most brilliant star of my days is extinguished, now that the prop and pillar of my house is broken, the blossom and adornment of my life withered, and the most precious treasure of my heart given up to decay?

But no! only his earthly part, his body, his tenement of dust has been returned unto dust whence it was taken, but his nobler being, his immortal part, his spirit continues to live with all its thoughts and feelings, with all its faithfulness and love. "*The dust returneth unto the earth as it was, and the spirit ascendeth unto God who gave it.*" Thus it

is written in Thy holy book. To this hope and promise I shall ever cleave. The thought that death cannot have altogether destroyed the bond of our hearts shall be my comfort in my mourning, balm to my wounded soul; and as my love follows him into yonder world, thus he will—I am convinced thereof—look down, with his love and his blessing, upon me (and my children whom he has left behind in orphaned condition); and as I raise my tear-moistened eye in fervent prayer to Thee, my God, to implore heavenly salvation *upon him*, he will, in return, invoke Thy mercy and grace *upon me* (*us*), and thus our souls will meet before Thy throne.

But unto Thee, O All-good Father in heaven! who art a father to the orphan and a judge to the widow in Thy sacred height, unto Thee I confide my life now deprived of its earthly protection, and my children bereaved of their guide and supporter. May Thy love surround me, Thine almightiness strengthen me, Thy wisdom enlighten me, that I may walk through life strong and courageous; that I may be enabled to fulfill the duties and obligations which are now my lot in double measure, with a manly spirit and a womanly heart, and to preside over my house with understanding and strength, and satisfy all its wants. Amen.

AT A HUSBAND'S GRAVE.

Thou sleepest beneath this tomb, dear husband; thou canst not hear me, neither canst thou see my tears. It has pleased God to remove thee from my love. My existence is now a void; joy and happiness have fled with thee, and I must bear the burden of life alone; for thy hand can no longer protect me, nor my heart repose on thine. All is cold and dreary, and I come to pour out my grief at thy grave.

Here, near thy lifeless clay, I seem to be, for a moment, united with thee again; thy spirit communes with mine, joins me in prayer, and comforts me with the hope of another existence.

May God support me in this heavy trial; may He in mercy pardon the words of bitterness which have escaped from my widowed heart. (*If there be children, say:* O God protect my bereaved children, deprived of their earthly father's care. Heavenly Father! extend Thy omnipotent protection, and inspire them with a love of duty and fidelity to our holy faith, and veneration for their father's memory.)

O my God! permit that my tears and sorrow may serve as an expiatory sacrifice for my sins, and for those of my family. May my endeavors to practise what is good atone for my errors, and be accepted in order to secure the salvation of my soul. May my husband, O God! repose in eternal peace, and may it be Thy holy will to unite those in heaven whom Thy blessing had joined on earth. Amen.

AT A WIFE'S GRAVE.

Beloved wife! my heart is sorely grieved; my whole earthly happiness lies entombed with thee. O thou! whose confiding love was the crown of my existence, whose kindness and devotion formed the joy of my heart! how can I avoid grieving, when I think that our children are deprived of thy tender affection and watchful care? O watch over them in thy blessed state! May thy memory guide them to do what is good, and be a protection for them against temptation and sin. May they always remember, and strive to imitate, thy gentleness, piety and virtue.

O God! grant unto her for whom I mourn, all the joys of eternity: grant that her soul may watch as a guardian angel over my bereaved children; remove every evil influence from them, and lead them in the way of righteousness, so that we may one day be all deemed worthy of being numbered among the blessed.

Repose in peace, beloved spirit! and may we meet in eternity. Amen.

AT A CHILD'S GRAVE.

Sweetly slumbering the darling of my heart rests here—my dear, early departed child; peace unto (*his—her*) soul! God of grace and mercy! forgive the depressed heart of a mother trembling in unutter-

able woe! Alas! the blossom that death broke off, was my happiness, and the life which was extinguished at Thy command, filled my heart with cheering hopes. By the side of my darling child, taken away so soon, I hope to enjoy the delight of existence in double measure, to endure more easily all sufferings, and to look towards my end without fear and trembling; for I hoped that (*his—her*) hand would close my eyes. But Thy thoughts, O Lord, are not our thoughts, Thy ways are not our ways. Thou hadst given me my beloved child, Thou hast taken (*him—her*) away, Thy name be praised! Yea, even from the depth of my grief I worship Thee with reverence. Whatever Thou doest is well done; Thou art our loving Father when Thou blessest and when Thou chastisest, when Thou givest and when Thou takest away, when Thou grantest life and when Thou sendest death. Thou woundest and bindest up again, Thou strikest, and Thy hand healeth again. Therefore, I pray unto Thee, Eternal God! fill Thou my saddened heart with consolation. Strengthen my confidence in Thine all-just ordinations, preserve me in obedience to Thy holy will. Forgive my sins, O Lord! and deliver me from all evil. Let the spirit of my child enjoy fullness of joy in Thy glorious habitation of peace; open unto it the source of truth and light, and let it ascend higher and higher in its everlasting salvation. Amen.

AT A CHILD'S GRAVE.

Here lies the hope and joy of my life. O God! to overcome thoughts of despair, and to learn resignation, I must pour out my heart to Thee, and implore thy pardon; for how grievously must I have sinned to be so sorely smitten! And yet, O Lord! I recognize Thy love, and humbly bow to Thy holy will; Thou hast deprived me of my child. Not for him, but for myself do I grieve. He is near Thee. (*For a child of tender age:* He has quitted this life before he could experience its sorrows or passions; his pure soul has returned to its Source, in the abode of purity and eternal joy.)

What Thou doest, Lord! is well done, Thou didst give, Thou hast taken away, blessed be Thy name. Yet, O Lord! it is for my own heart that I mourn, it still bleeds at its bitter loss. I strive to submit with resignation; yet my strength will sometimes fail to bear the burden of my grief. Aid me, O God! for Thou knowest the strength of my faith and trust in Thee. Thou wilt not condemn a father's (*mother's*) tears; for Thou, God! didst endow me with tender affections.

O Thou! beloved child, who, although so young, didst awaken so much joy and love, receive this tribute of thy parent's sorrow. Thou art now among the angels that serve near the throne of our Heavenly Father; yet will thy memory endure to the last

day of my life, when I shall hope to join thee in the dwelling-place of the Most High.

May thy dust repose in peace, and thy spirit enjoy eternal beatitude. Amen.

____

AT A BROTHER'S OR SISTER'S GRAVE.

Full of loving recollections I draw nigh unto the grave of my beloved (*brother—sister*) whose memory can never cease. Oh! that thou hast departed from me, that thou hast been taken from me, with whom I was united by the most tender bonds of blood and love. My spirit wanders back to the days of our childhood which we passed together, in joy and sorrow, with the most fervent devotion and attachment, when, faithfully clinging to each other, we entered upon the paths of life, and strove towards our aim, and endured together, with the most sincere mutual sympathy, all suffering and trials. Verily, life was of value to us because we enjoyed it together. And though now and then differences of opinion and intentions would separate us, how quickly would we again extend our hands to each other, and forget all! All at once thou wast taken from me—relentless death tore thee from my arms. Thy picture stands before me and fills me with unutterable woe and longing. Alas! thou shalt never return unto me, and I must wait for the time when we shall be re-united. Then thy spirit—as once thy hand,—will

seize mine, and lead me up, and show me the way unto purer light, unto higher joys.—O Lord! may my (*brother's—sister's*) spirit have attained to eternal peace, that (*his—her*) heart, satisfied by Thy river of love, be filled with the highest clearness and cheered by the highest salvation! Peace be unto this consecrated spot that contains these remains. Amen.

AT A BROTHER'S OR SISTER'S GRAVE.

May peace be thine, dear friend of my youth! What gentle memories and bitter regrets cluster around this tomb. Alas! death claimed thee too soon, and removed thee too early from those who loved thee. What grief! to think that we, whom one roof sheltered, one mother nourished, the same hearts cherished and the same hands blessed, are forever separated! We were so happy together; thy friendship was so sweet a support. Alas! thy departure has turned our joy into mourning. Nothing on earth is lasting. I grieve in my selfishness at having lost thee; but thou art happy near our Heavenly Father, and this thought will inspire me with courage and resignation, as likewise the glorious hope of meeting thee again in a better world, where eternal joy awaits the righteous.

O my God! grant unto my brother's (*sister's*) soul the happiness of the righteous; grant that, purified by death, he (*she*) may rejoice in the beatitude of Thy divine presence. Amen.

AT A GRANDPARENT'S GRAVE.

With deep veneration I approach thy tomb to do homage to thy memory, dear grandfather (*grandmother*), and recall to my mind thy many virtues. May this tribute of love and respect be a worthy offering to thy memory, which shall keep me in the path of rectitude, that I may follow the example of piety and goodness thou hast left to our family. I will strive, with the help of God, to leave a like heritage to my children.

May my vow to honor thy memory by the practice of virtue be acceptable to God, and may He aid me in my righteous endeavors. Amen.

AT A FRIEND'S OR RELATIVE'S GRAVE.

Mayest thou rest in peace, dear friend! Death has severed the tie that united us in this life, to be renewed everlastingly in a happier world, whither I shall one day follow thee.

Now, faithful to thy memory, I implore God to grant repose unto thy soul; and to vouchsafe to me · the grace of a reunion when His holy will shall call me hence.

My God! permit that the soul of him (*her*) for whom I mourn, freed from earth's painful struggles, dangers and difficulties, and purified through thy mercy, may share the joys of the blessed in eternity. Amen.

ON SETTING A TOMBSTONE.

"A mere shadow are our days upon the earth."
(Job viii, 9.) Naught is left to me of him who has
gone "to the valley of the shadow of death" but a
stone bearing his name. This is all we have to mark
the spot where his mortal remains are laid, to re-
mind us of what we too shall soon become. In the
grave all our efforts end. Here is nothing but a
fragile stone or a nameless grave, to recall to us the
memory of those whom we leave behind, unless we
sow the seed of goodness and useful deeds in our
earthly career, the fruits of which we shall reap in
heaven.

O thou! who sleepest in the dust, this monument
was not needed to recall thy name, for thy precious
memory is enthroned in the hearts of many; but thy
gentle qualities and kind friendship have so endeared
thy image to my soul, that death alone can efface
the remembrance of the loss I have sustained in thy
decease.

May thy body rest in peace. Lord! in setting
this stone to the memory of...........I beseech
Thee to grant repose to his (her) soul, give him (her)
the peace of the righteous, and admit him (her) to
the joy of contemplating Thy divine presence.

Vouchsafe Thy mercy to me, O Lord! that my
spirit may one day also enjoy eternal beatitude, and
make my memory worthy of being honored and preserved among those whom I shall leave behind. Amen.

ON LEAVING THE CEMETERY.

"Then shall the dust return to the earth whence it came, and the spirit shall return unto God who gave it." (Ezek. xii, 7.) Peace be with you, all whom death has united in this field, the last home of so many departed ones. Peace be with your souls, which have been recalled by the voice of God to eternal life. Amen.

THE END.

DEATH RECORD.

DEATH RECORD.